NIGHT OF THE VAMPIRE

Nate is such a happy guy, Irene observed. He thinks he lucked out and found the girl of his dreams.

She kissed him gently on the neck.

Then slid her fangs down.

She prepared to sink them into his throat.

The need surged through her.

Hungry, she thought. So very, very hungry.

Her fangs touched the softness of Nate's neck.

Books by R. L. Stine

FEAR STREET
THE NEW GIRL
THE SURPRISE PARTY
THE OVERNIGHT
MISSING
THE WRONG NUMBER
THE SLEEPWALKER
HAUNTED
HALLOWEEN PARTY
THE STEPSISTER
SKI WEEKEND
THE FIRE GAME
LIGHTS OUT
THE SECRET BEDROOM
THE KNIFE
PROM QUEEN
FIRST DATE
THE BEST FRIEND
THE CHEATER
SUNBURN
THE NEW BOY
THE DARE
BAD DREAMS
DOUBLE DATE
THE THRILL CLUB
ONE EVIL SUMMER
THE MIND READER
WRONG NUMBER 2
TRUTH OR DARE
DEAD END
FINAL GRADE
SWITCHED
COLLEGE WEEKEND
THE STEPSISTER 2
WHAT HOLLY HEARD
THE FACE
SECRET ADMIRER
THE PERFECT DATE
THE CONFESSION
THE BOY NEXT DOOR

FEAR STREET SUPER CHILLERS
PARTY SUMMER
SILENT NIGHT
GOODNIGHT KISS
BROKEN HEARTS
SILENT NIGHT 2
THE DEAD LIFEGUARD
CHEERLEADERS: THE NEW EVIL
BAD MOONLIGHT
THE NEW YEAR'S PARTY
GOODNIGHT KISS 2

THE FEAR STREET SAGA
THE BETRAYAL
THE SECRET
THE BURNING

FEAR STREET CHEERLEADERS
THE FIRST EVIL
THE SECOND EVIL
THE THIRD EVIL

99 FEAR STREET: THE HOUSE OF EVIL
THE FIRST HORROR
THE SECOND HORROR
THE THIRD HORROR

THE CATALUNA CHRONICLES
THE EVIL MOON
THE DARK SECRET
THE DEADLY FIRE

FEAR STREET SAGAS
A NEW FEAR
HOUSE OF WHISPERS

OTHER NOVELS
HOW I BROKE UP WITH ERNIE
PHONE CALLS
CURTAINS
BROKEN DATE

Availabe from **ARCHWAY** Paperbacks

Goodnight Kiss 2

A Parachute Press Book

AN ARCHWAY PAPERBACK
Published by POCKET BOOKS
New York London Toronto Sydney Tokyo Singapore

This book is a work of fiction. Names, characters, places and incidents are products of the author's imagination or are used fictitiously. Any resemblance to actual events or locales or persons, living or dead, is entirely coincidental.

AN ARCHWAY PAPERBACK *Original*

An Archway Paperback published by
POCKET BOOKS, a division of Simon & Schuster Inc.
1230 Avenue of the Americas, New York, NY 10020

ISBN: 0-671-52969-2

First Archway Paperback printing July 1996

10 9 8 7 6 5 4 3 2 1

Cover art by Bill Schmidt

Printed in the U.S.A.

IL 6+

Goodnight Kiss 2

Prologue

A NICE TIME

A pale moon floated high over the beach at Sandy Hollow as Diana walked beside Eric. The wet sand felt cold under her feet. Diana took Eric's hand. "I love the beach at night," she murmured.

"Huh? What did you say?" Eric asked. He seemed distracted.

"Nothing. Come on." Pulling him toward the waves that broke gently on the sand, Diana began to walk faster.

The beach is so peaceful at night, she thought. So perfect for what I must do.

The stars gleamed, silvery against the clear black sky. It was at least an hour before dawn. Diana had plenty of time.

She studied Eric's face. His hair was black and

shaggy, his eyes dark and serious. Her gaze lingered on his throat, on the smooth flesh just below his jaw.

Any moment now, she thought. Any moment.

"It's late," Eric said. "I really should go home."

"Not afraid of the dark, are you?" Diana teased.

"Of course not."

"Then what's the hurry?"

"I had a crazy day. I'd like to get a little sleep before the sun comes up."

Diana stopped walking and peered down the dark beach. "Look!" she cried. "Someone left a beach umbrella. Let's sit down. Just for a minute?"

"But it's so late," Eric protested.

Diana hurried to the umbrella and dropped onto the sand beneath it. "Come on," she urged. "We've got our own private spot."

Eric joined her. She pulled him to her and kissed him. Just once. Quickly. His lips felt cool on hers. As cool as the night air.

"I really have to get home," Eric whispered.

"You're not going home, Eric."

For a moment, he said nothing, his face a frozen silhouette against the star-filled sky. "What are you talking about?" he finally asked.

"I brought you here to die."

He laughed. "Is this a joke?"

"No, Eric. It's no joke. A vampire murdered my cousin last summer. She wasn't just my cousin, Eric. She was also my best friend. I want all vampires to die."

Eric's fangs slid down. "You lose," he snarled.

"No. *You* lose," Diana snapped.

His eyes glowed with rage and hunger. He reached for her.

Diana rolled away. She yanked the beach umbrella from the sand. The special umbrella she had made for tonight.

Eric came after her, moonlight flashing in his eyes.

The umbrella top slid across the sand as Diana yanked the pole off.

"I can already taste your blood, the sweet nectar!" Eric proclaimed.

"Don't count on it," Diana replied.

Eric groaned as she jammed the pole's sharp wooden tip through his heart. His eyes bulged wide in shock. "No!" he gasped. "No. You *can't!*"

He collapsed onto the sand.

The glow in his eyes faded.

His body shriveled. Slowly at first, then faster, his legs shrinking beneath his jeans. His arms dissolving. His skin flaking, blowing away in the wind.

Until a skeleton lay sprawled on the sand in Eric's clothes.

Bones. White bones.

Then dust.

Diana stirred the dust around with her hand until it disappeared into the beach sand.

"Goodbye, Eric," she murmured. "I had a very nice time."

PART ONE

PARTY TIME

Chapter 1

VAMPIRE ISLAND

"There's the Pizza Cove," Billy Naughton announced, pointing to a small restaurant across the street. "Excellent sausage and mushroom pizza."

Jay Windley nodded.

"Best pizza in town," Nate Stanton agreed as he ran a hand through his sandy hair. "I ate it every night last summer. Really. I mean, *every* night."

Jay nodded again.

Billy glanced around for other Sandy Hollow landmarks to point out. He had decided to spend the first night showing his best friend around. After all, he had spent all of last summer here, and Jay had never been to Sandy Hollow before.

Jay's friend Nate seemed kind of boring. Nate

and his family had been at Sandy Hollow last summer. But Billy didn't remember much about them.

Maybe I was too busy with Joelle to notice anyone else, Billy thought.

"I don't like the Pizza Cove," announced Lynette, Nate's little sister. Billy had a feeling Lynette would be tagging along all summer. It was only the first night, and already Mrs. Stanton had made Nate take her with them.

"Who cares what you like?" Nate teased her. "You'd like Gummi Worms on your pizza!"

Billy felt the salty dampness of the ocean breeze on his cheeks. The wind ruffled his long, black hair. He shook himself out of his daze. "It gets cold here at night," he commented.

"No kidding," Jay muttered, shivering. The ocean breeze plastered his light brown hair against his cheek.

"It's fun even when it's cold," Nate declared. "This is going to be an awesome summer. Except for work."

Billy groaned. "Don't remind me." He turned to Jay. "What are you going to do while we're at work, Jay? Hang out with your parents?"

Jay laughed. "No way. I'm going to hang out at the beach and get a killer tan. But I'll be thinking about you poor working guys all the time."

"Yeah, right." Nate gave him a shove. Jay stumbled into a woman passing by.

Billy laughed. Nate was a big guy. Big and strong. He was nearly twice Jay's size.

Jay's taste in friends really changed while I was away this past year, Billy thought. He never used to hang out with jocks.

"The only thing I want to do this summer is meet girls," Jay said.

"This is the place, man," Nate told him. "I had three girlfriends last summer!"

Jay grinned. "If there are so many girls, how come we haven't met any yet?"

"He said there were a lot of girls," Billy replied. "He didn't say they'd be interested in *you,* Jay."

Nate laughed loudly and slapped Billy a high-five.

"All my friends think Nate's a jerk," Lynette announced.

Nate's smile disappeared. "Why don't you go play in the ocean, Lynette?"

Lynette skipped happily along behind him. "My friends *all* think you're a total jerk," she repeated.

"Who cares what your friends think?" Nate grumbled. "I'm talking about real girls—not little kids in elementary school."

Lynette stuck her tongue out.

Billy rolled his eyes at Nate in sympathy.

"Wow, look!" Lynette exclaimed. "An ice-cream place."

Billy followed the direction of her gaze. She had discovered Swanny's, the ice-cream parlor and video arcade.

"Ice cream!" Lynette demanded, tugging her brother's sleeve. "Ice cream!"

Nate snorted. "Maybe later."

They drifted down Main Street, then crossed to the other side and headed back the way they had come.

Only a few shoppers at the Mini Market, Billy observed. The summer season had barely begun. In a few days the Mini Market and every other shop in Sandy Hollow would be crowded night and day with summer people.

"This has *got* to be a great summer," Billy declared. "I deserve it after the year I had."

"Yeah, it was so weird with you being in that hospital," Jay replied. "I couldn't even visit you."

"So what?" Nate put in. "Look on the bright side, Billy. You got to miss a whole year of school!"

"Well, I'm better now," Billy declared. "And ready to party—big time!"

Nate stuck his hand in the air and Billy high-fived him.

"How are your jobs starting out?" Jay asked.

Billy and Nate groaned in unison.

"Mine's not too bad," Billy replied. "At least I'm outside all day on the boat. My boss says sometimes rich guys charter it to go deep-sea fishing. Maybe I'll get some big tips."

"At least you *wanted* a job," Nate complained. "When my dad found out the golf course needed help, he said I'd do it—without even asking me! I wanted to party this summer, not kill weeds and replace divots."

"Daddy says it will be good for you," Lynette chimed in. "Because you're a lazy bum."

Nate glared at her.

"Well, I'm not going to let work keep me from having a good time," Billy declared. "I can work all day and party all night. Who needs to sleep?"

"I can party all night, too," Nate agreed. "Bring on the girls."

Jay laughed. "Get serious. In two days you'll both be totally wiped."

"Not me," Nate insisted. "No way!"

Billy was only half listening to his friends. The sound of surf in the distance had caught his attention. "Hey, let's check out the beach!" he suggested.

He led the way off Main Street to locate a boardwalk that ran to the beach. The old wooden steps leading down from the dunes groaned and sagged under their weight.

They had the beach to themselves. Billy knew it wouldn't last. By the end of the week, the beach would be jammed with sunbathers and swimmers and kids making sand castles. And at night there would be clambakes and bonfires and parties.

I can't wait, Billy thought. I can't wait to get started.

"You're right, man, this is awesome," Jay agreed.

Billy glanced around. The crests of the waves glowed white in the silvery moonlight. Billy could see a stone jetty in the distance, stretching out from the shore until it disappeared into the sea.

"What's that?" Jay cried.

Billy jumped. He heard Lynette gasp.

The sky suddenly filled with noise. Flapping. Fluttering. Above them. In front of them. Behind them.

"Look!" Nate shouted, pointing toward the jetty.

Billy saw them. Bats. Dozens of them, flying low over the stone jetty.

A chill slid down Billy's spine. He stared at the

bats. So many of them, he thought. How can there be so many?

"Awesome," Jay whispered.

Lynette squeezed past Billy and hid behind Nate.

The bats fluttered up, blocking the moonlight, darkening the beach. Then they flew out to sea and disappeared.

"Where did they go?" Lynette asked in a tiny voice.

"To the island," Billy answered. "There's an island close to shore. Nobody lives there anymore. The bats use the abandoned houses."

"Bat island," Jay said. "Sounds like a place in a horror movie."

"The local people call it Vampire Island," Nate corrected him. "It's covered with burned-out houses. That's why no one lives there."

Jay laughed. "*Vampire* Island? Give me a break!"

"Some people say vampires lived there—in the abandoned houses," Billy explained. "Some high school kids went out there after a graduation party. They dared one another to find the vampires and destroy them. Two kids found a coffin and set it on fire."

Lynette shivered. She moved closer to Nate.

"The fire killed the vampire," Billy continued. "But when the kids tried to leave the island, other vampires followed them. The kids tried to set them on fire, too. All the houses burned, and none of the kids ever came back from the island.

"Some people say they died in the fire with the vampires. But other people believe that the vampires got them. So now nobody ever goes there."

"How many kids were there?" Lynette asked.

"Six. I heard that three of them tried to row away. But the vampires changed into bats and flew to the boat and killed them."

Nate laughed. "What a dumb story. Does anyone really believe it?"

"A lot of people do," Billy replied softly.

They stood silently, staring at the rock jetty.

Finally Billy turned away from the rolling, dark ocean. "Let's go back to town," he suggested, shivering.

His friends immediately agreed. Billy knew they had been spooked by the bats—and by his story. Lynette grabbed Nate's sleeve and wouldn't let go.

"How am I going to meet any girls with my little sister always tagging along?" Nate grumbled.

"If you don't want me here, I'll go home," Lynette declared.

"No!" Nate cried. "No way."

"Why not?"

"Because Mom will *kill* me."

"Buy me an ice cream, or I'll tell Mom you tried to lose me!"

"But that's blackmail!" Nate protested.

Billy chuckled. "She's got you, Nate."

"I'd buy her the ice-cream cone if I were you," Jay told him.

Nate gave in. "Okay. Okay. Ice cream."

Billy had to laugh. Nate was a big, tough-looking guy. And his little sister knew exactly how to push him around.

They walked along the beach in silence. But as Billy stepped onto the stairs leading up to the boardwalk, Lynette let out a piercing scream.

"No!" she wailed. "Let him go! Let him go! Nooo!"

Chapter 2

DOGGIE GOES FLYING

Billy gasped as he saw why Lynette was screaming.

Down the beach, two enormous bats attacked a small black dog. Terrified, the dog spun in circles, snapping at them.

But the bats attacked viciously. Swooping from the sky, screeching and snapping their jaws.

One flapping bat landed on the dog's back. It sank its teeth into the little dog's flesh.

The dog let out a yelp of pain.

The other bat swooped onto the dog's neck, biting deeply.

Billy watched, stunned, as the bats gripped the dog in their jaws and began flapping their wings frantically.

The dog twisted helplessly, letting out cry after cry.

This is impossible, Billy thought. *Bats can't do this.*

Their wings beat the air furiously. They lifted the yelping dog off the ground.

The animal struggled, twisting one way, then the other. But the bats held on.

Slowly they lifted the dog.

A foot off the beach.

Two feet.

Still higher.

Flapping hard, they moved toward the ocean.

Billy felt rooted to the sand, unable to move. Unable to take his eyes off the horrifying sight.

He heard Lynette's sobs. Saw her run after the squirming, howling dog.

"Lynette—come back!" Billy cried. He sprinted after her. Over the sound of his own breathing, Billy heard Nate and Jay running close behind him. Their footsteps sounded hollow on the damp sand.

Billy quickly overtook Lynette. He was gaining on the bats. They seemed to be having trouble carrying such a heavy load. Flapping furiously, they moved slowly along the shore.

The dog kicked its legs and howled.

Billy ran harder. Nate and Jay beside him now.

"Stop them!" Lynette screamed.

From the corner of his eye, Billy saw Jay stumble. Jay toppled facefirst into the sand.

Billy didn't slow down. Nate still ran beside him. They were close to the bats.

The dog wailed in fright. Blood poured from where the bats had ripped its throat.

The bats beat the air with their wings.

Billy ran until he was directly underneath them. He reached up. Tried to grab the dog. Missed by a couple of inches.

Nate jumped too. And missed.

Got to jump higher, Billy thought.

He leaped again. Missed again.

The bats flapped furiously.

Flying faster now.

Pulling away from Billy.

Billy ran as fast as he could. Nate chugged along beside him.

Something cold and wet grabbed Billy's legs. Swept him off balance.

Billy glanced down. He had run into the ocean. A tall wave splashed over him, pushing him back, startling him with its cold.

Billy saw Nate splashing in knee-deep water, still chasing the bats. A moment later, Nate began bobbing with the waves as they rolled in to shore. Nate's feet, Billy realized, were no longer touching bottom.

"Nate!" Billy shouted. "Come back! There's nothing we can do!"

Nate swam to Billy's side. They watched as the bats and dog became a ghastly silhouette against the moon. Growing smaller and smaller. Until they disappeared.

They're taking the dog to the island, Billy thought. Taking it home to feed on it. Sickened, he stared out toward the island. Feelings of horror and disgust filled him.

Just wait, he thought bitterly. I know you're not really bats. I know what you are. And I'll destroy you. I promise, before summer is over, I'll destroy you all.

Chapter 3

DINNERTIME

Lynette no longer felt like having ice cream. She just wanted to go home.

Billy, Jay, and Nate led the way along the path that led to the summer condos their families had rented. They talked quietly among themselves. They didn't want to frighten Lynette more.

"Those were vampires," Billy murmured.

"Vampire bats?" Jay asked. "I never knew they were so strong."

"Not vampire bats," Billy corrected him. "Vampires who turn into bats."

Jay snorted.

"Yeah, right," Nate muttered. "And Frankenstein rents the beach house next to mine."

"You saw what they did," Billy whispered. "You really think ordinary bats could do that?"

Lynette began to bawl again. "Are they going to kill the dog?" she wailed. She had been listening after all.

"Nice job, Billy," Nate muttered. He tried to comfort his sister.

"Look, I'm sorry, but it's true," Billy replied. "You have to believe me. Those were not ordinary bats."

"I don't believe in vampires," Jay declared. "Because they're a pain in the neck!" He roared at his own joke.

"It's not funny," Lynette cried. "It's scary!"

"She's right," Billy said. "And if you don't listen to me, you could be in a lot of danger."

"From vampires?" Jay rolled his eyes.

"From vampires," Billy repeated. He stared hard at Jay, trying to convince his best friend that he was serious.

Jay frowned. "Um, Billy, it's kind of hard to believe that vampires really exist."

He thinks I'm messed up, Billy realized. He gazed at the troubled faces of his friends. Noticed the glances they exchanged.

They both think I'm crazy, he thought. But I can't blame them. I would have thought the same thing . . . before last summer.

The memory tortured Billy even now.

But he was here to put an end to the evil in Sandy Hollow. If his friends were going to help him, they had to know the truth about last summer.

The truth about Sandy Hollow.

"I had a girlfriend last summer," Billy explained. "Her name was Joelle. I met her the first week I was here, and we spent the whole summer together."

"What happened?" Jay asked. His eyes shone with interest.

Billy took a deep breath. "The vampires killed her. They flew from the vampire island as bats. Then they returned to their human form and killed Joelle. They drank her blood until she died."

His friends stared at him. Billy could see that they didn't believe him.

"I know it sounds insane," Billy admitted. "But that's what happened. I saw the bite marks on Joelle's neck."

"Maybe they were mosquito bites?" Jay asked.

"I know what a mosquito bite looks like," Billy snapped. "These were different. Bigger and deeper."

Nate rubbed his chin. "Was Joelle the girl they found on the beach?"

Billy nodded.

"They said she drowned," Nate argued. "Nobody mentioned vampires."

Billy could tell from the three faces staring at

him that, no matter what he said, none of them would believe him. Nate wore a smug grin that seemed to say, *You don't really think I'm going to fall for this, do you?* Jay revealed no emotion at all.

Billy felt his anger rising. He forced himself to stay calm. "Jay, I didn't tell you the whole story about why I missed a year of school," he continued. "The reason you couldn't visit me is because I wasn't in a regular hospital. It was a mental hospital."

Billy lowered his eyes to the ground. Now they'll think I'm *totally* nuts, he thought.

He pressed on. "I was pretty messed up by what happened to Joelle. Shock trauma, they called it. I guess I—"

"Then I don't get it," Jay interrupted. "Why did you come back here? If something like that happened to me, I'd never want to see this place again."

Billy took a deep breath. "I came back to find the vampires who killed Joelle—to hunt them down and destroy them."

"Are there really vampires?" Lynette asked in a small voice.

"Yes," Billy replied.

"No," Nate declared.

"What about the dog?" Billy demanded.

"That was weird," Jay admitted. "But all we

know about bats is what we learned in biology. Maybe the bats they've got here are different. Maybe they fly off with dogs all the time."

Nate chuckled.

"It's not funny!" Billy exploded. "You didn't see what happened to Joelle!"

He spun away from them and started to stalk away.

The others hurried to catch up with him. "Whoa. Calm down," Jay urged. "We came here to party—remember?"

"Yeah, man," Nate agreed. "We want to get some sun and meet some major babes."

"It's too early to go home," Jay protested. "Let's head back to Main Street. Check out the action."

None of them believe me, Billy realized. But I'll make them believe if it's the last thing I do.

April Blair hid in the shadows. Waiting. Watching. Two bats landed on the soft sand a few feet from where she stood. Remaining perfectly still, she studied them.

They began to spin.

Faster and faster.

Until they became two whirling columns.

Stretching. Growing longer, higher.

Slowing, taking shape.

Developing shoulders, arms, legs.

Heads. Faces.

In seconds, two girls stood where the bats had whirled.

Awesome hair, April thought, gazing at the redheaded girl. So long and full. And it actually shimmers in the moonlight.

She turned her eyes to the other girl. A mass of golden curls framed her smooth, pale face. The curls swayed gently when she moved her head.

"I need human nectar," the one with red hair moaned. "Dog nectar is too thin. It isn't satisfying. And the dog put up too much of a fight. Humans don't resist the way animals do."

"Well, human nectar is in season," the other declared. "The summer people are all arriving."

"Just in time. I'm so hungry!"

It's time to show myself, April thought. She stepped from the shadows and moved toward the two vampires.

"Hey!" yelled the red-haired girl. The vampires advanced.

April waited for them. Met their eyes.

"We won't have to be hungry much longer," the redheaded one declared. "The nectar came to us. Home delivery."

April stopped. She watched the vampires' fangs slide down. Needle-sharp points. Ready to penetrate her neck. The hunger made their breath come in rapid, excited hisses.

The redheaded girl reached for her.

"Don't be stupid," April snapped. "Don't you recognize one of your own?"

They hesitated.

"I was here last summer," April told them. "And I became one of you."

"Who remembers the summer people?" the redheaded girl asked disdainfully. "They're all just food to me."

"All just food," the blond one repeated.

April saw the hunger in their eyes, the unquenchable yearning for nectar.

"Wait. I think I remember you," the blond girl declared. "It was Gabri who turned you into an Immortal, wasn't it?"

April nodded. "That's right," she agreed. "Gabri did it."

"What's your name?" the blond vampire asked.

"April Blair."

"I'm Irene," the blond girl told her. "And this is Kylie."

Kylie grinned at April, showing her fangs.

April realized that Irene was studying her, sizing her up. But Kylie seemed interested in only one thing. Nectar. Her eyes glowed with hunger. A glistening drop of saliva trickled from the corner of her mouth.

"Why are we standing around here?" Kylie

asked hungrily. "I need the nectar. I need it *now.*"

"Let's go," Irene agreed.

They climbed the dune that rose to street level.

"I'm so glad summer is finally here," Irene murmured.

"I hate the winter," Kylie grumbled. "There is hardly anybody around. I get so hungry."

They reached the street. April waited as Kylie checked her appearance, adjusted the black scrunchie in her hair, smoothed her short denim skirt.

Irene caught April's eye and smirked. "Kylie thinks she has to look good to attract the nectar."

April shook her head. "Why don't you just cloud their minds?" she asked Kylie. "Make them helpless and drink all the nectar you want."

"It's more fun this way," Kylie replied. "I'm ready. Let's go." She strode onto the sidewalk near the dune.

April gazed at the scene as they wandered toward Main Street. People strolled along the sidewalks. A man and woman with a toddler. Two girls in Hard Rock Cafe T-shirts. A gray-haired couple walking slowly, gazing into the shop windows.

"Nectar," Kylie whispered.

Irene gripped April's arm. "Look."

Following Irene's gaze, April spotted three

boys across the street. A young girl tagged along behind them.

That guy is pretty cute, April thought.

The boy was tall, with long, dark hair. He pointed to something. He seemed to be showing the others around town.

Look at me, April thought, staring hard at the boy. Turn this way and look at me.

The tall boy shifted his gaze in April's direction. He stopped short, pulling his friends to a halt. All three boys turned to stare.

Kylie tossed her red hair and chuckled. "They're so easy to control, aren't they?" she murmured.

"Dinnertime," April proclaimed hungrily. "Let's go get them."

Chapter 4

DESSERT

"Whoa. Watch out!" April cried as Kylie pushed past her.

But the redheaded girl ignored her. She stepped up to the tall, black-haired boy. "Hi," she said. "You guys here for the summer?"

Wow, April thought. I guess we know which one she wants.

"Yeah. I'm here for the next two months," the boy replied.

Kylie cocked her head and smiled, her red hair tumbling over her shoulder. "I'll be here until Labor Day," she told him.

April realized that Irene had started talking to the big, athletic-looking boy. That left the short, thin one for her.

"Hi, I'm April."

"Oh, uh, my name's Jay."

Seems nervous, April thought. "Where are you from?" she asked.

"Uh . . . Holcomb. All of us are from there."

"I'm from Shadyside."

"Never been there," he replied, abruptly displaying a big goofy grin. "Is it nice?"

"It will never make the list of the top five hundred most fabulous places to live!"

Jay laughed. "Neither will Holcomb."

Good, April thought, he's starting to loosen up a little. Jay introduced her to his friends, Nate and Billy. And to the little girl, Lynette.

Kylie's tinkling laugh caught April's attention. She turned to see the girl slip her arm through Billy's.

Kylie tried to pull him away from the others. But Billy seemed to resist. He looked very uncomfortable.

April smiled to herself. Never thought I'd see any boy resist the charms of someone like Kylie, she thought.

She turned to Irene and Nate. At least Irene is doing well, she thought.

Nate seemed much more interested than Billy. He was grinning nonstop at Irene.

These boys will do, April decided. We can keep them around for a while.

"How would you guys like to be in a play?" she asked. All three reacted with surprise.

"Tryouts are this week at the summer theater," April continued. "A lot of kids have already joined the theater group. They've made sets and everything."

"What play are you doing?" Jay asked.

"Night of the Vampire," April replied. She saw Irene and Kylie glance at each other. She smiled at the boys. "We're really short on guys," she added. "We're *always* short on guys."

"What's it about?" Nate asked.

"Might be about vampires," Jay teased him.

"Duh. I know, I know," Nate grumbled. "I mean, what is the story like?"

"It's about two vampires who fall in love with their victims," April explained. "It's a comedy."

Irene laughed.

"It sounds kind of cool," Nate said. "But Billy and I both have jobs."

"No problem," April assured him. "Rehearsals are always at night—all the performances, too. A lot of us . . . can't make it during the day."

"You said a lot of kids are in the play?" Billy asked.

April turned to him in surprise. Why did he

sound so suspicious? "Yeah," she answered. "A lot."

"Then I'm in," Billy declared. "I really want to meet people this summer."

April narrowed her eyes at Billy. What's his problem? she wondered.

"Come on, let's walk," Kylie urged, tugging on Billy's arm.

They strolled along Main Street. Irene stopped in front of the Beach Emporium window. "Nice bikinis, huh?" she said to Billy.

He shrugged.

Irene shook her head. "A little too wild for me."

"For *you,* yeah," Kylie sneered. "You're so . . . out of it."

"It's called good taste," Irene shot back. "But I wouldn't expect you to know about that."

Kylie and Irene have only one thing in common, April decided. The need for nectar. It will be a long summer hanging out with them.

"I hear there are a lot of wild parties here during the summer," Kylie said to Billy.

"There are usually parties and bonfires on the beach," Billy replied. "They get pretty wild sometimes."

"I love to party," Kylie murmured, staring into his eyes.

Billy walked on without replying.

Wow, April thought. Kylie can *not* seem to get him interested. Not many guys would pass up a chance with a girl as beautiful as Kylie. What is his deal?

She turned back to Jay. "Have you come here before?"

He gave her another big lopsided grin. "Uh, well . . . no. It's my first time."

"Don't be so nervous," April teased him. "I don't bite!"

Jay blushed a bright red. "I'm not nervous," he insisted. He gave her a shy smile.

He's actually kind of cute, April decided. I guess I'll stick with him. Kylie wants Billy, anyway.

April glanced at the redheaded vampire. She was still holding onto Billy's arm. And he still appeared bothered by it.

Billy is too suspicious, April decided. Kylie will have a hard time with him. I'm better off with Jay.

"I want to go home." Lynette's shrill voice cut into April's thoughts.

"Now?" Nate growled.

"Mom said you had to get me back before eleven."

Nate glanced at his watch and sighed. "Okay."

"We'd better go, too," Billy declared. "Nate and I have to work tomorrow."

"Can we get together again?" Nate asked Irene.

"I'm going to try out for the vampire play," Irene answered. "Maybe I'll see you there."

"Excellent!" Nate beamed.

"I think I'll try out too," Kylie declared. She gazed up at Billy. "It's my kind of play."

Billy didn't answer. Jay and Nate said good-bye. The three boys left, with Lynette tagging along beside her brother.

Kylie sighed. "I'm so thirsty. I like that Billy. I wanted to sink my fangs into him."

"He didn't seem to like you too much," April observed.

Kylie whipped around to face April, her eyes flashing with anger. "It's because I'm so hungry! I tried to cloud his mind, but I was too weak. But tonight I'm going to drink *someone's* nectar! Anyone's."

"Take it easy," Irene cautioned. "We have all summer. If you drink too much and kill one of them, the summer people will be all upset."

"Who cares if they get upset?" Kylie demanded. "Do you think I care about hurting their feelings?"

"If too many dead bodies turn up," April pointed out, "the police will close the beach. The summer people will leave. All the food will go away."

"I hate taking just sips," Kylie complained. "Sips are never enough."

"But if you drink too much blood and kill them, there will be no nectar at all. They might even get wise to us—and hunt us while we sleep!" Irene insisted. "We have to take sips."

Kylie let out a growl. She shifted her smoldering eyes to April. "You sure were coming on to Jay. You're hungry too, aren't you?"

April nodded. "Starving."

"Remember," Irene warned. "Just take sips. After three sips, they become one of us. They become an Immortal. But that's the way it has to be. Don't kill anyone."

"Unless *they* attack you," Kylie added. She gave a hungry moan. "Why did those boys have to go home so early?"

"They'll be back tomorrow," April promised.

"It will be so boring, just taking sips from them." Kylie sighed.

April nodded. "I wanted to drink Jay up. Drink until he was dry!"

"Hey! How about a bet?" Kylie suggested. "That will make things more interesting! First one to turn one of those three boys into an Immortal wins."

April giggled. "You're on."

"Okay," Irene agreed. "It will be fun."

"I've won already," April declared. "Jay is so ripe, so ready . . ."

"Billy won't resist me next time," Kylie insisted. "This will be an easy bet to win."

The tips of Kylie's fangs slid into view. Her eyes blazed. April had never seen such intense hunger before.

"Kylie!" Irene snapped. "Watch it! We're on Main Street!"

Kylie's fangs disappeared. "I'm so hungry," she whispered. "So terribly hungry."

"What will be the prize if we win?" April asked.

"Yes," Kylie said, "what will I win for making Billy one of us?"

Irene chuckled. "I've got it. The perfect prize. At the end of the summer, the winner can have the other two boys for dessert!"

Chapter 5

VAMPIRE TRYOUTS

Billy leaned against the stage and gazed out at the kids who had shown up for play tryouts. There were about thirty of them—everybody talking at once, laughing, telling jokes, teasing each other.

Which ones? he thought.

He studied their faces. Were any of them vampires? Did the cute girl in the front row sleep in a coffin all day because direct sunlight would kill her?

How about the two boys giving each other high-fives?

Where are they? he wondered. Where are the vampires who killed Joelle?

A short, round woman with her blond hair in a bun strode onto the stage. "All right, everybody!" she shouted, trying to be heard over all the noise. "Let me have your attention."

The noise slowly died down. "I'm Ms. Aaronson," she announced. "I run the community theater here at Sandy Hollow. And I'm thrilled to see so many young people here."

Billy tuned her out as she talked about the play. He stared intently at the other kids in the auditorium seats. Each friendly smile could hide sharp fangs, he knew. Each strange face could belong to a monster.

Ms. Aaronson cleared her throat. Billy glanced up at her again. "Let's see," she said. "Ah, here we are. Jay Windley, you're first. Please read from the script."

Jay stepped forward, looking very tense. Billy couldn't help smiling when Jay gave Ms. Aaronson one of his lopsided grins.

Jay took a deep breath and began reading. He was usually pretty soft-spoken, but now his voice sounded deep and powerful as he said the lines.

He's pretty good, Billy thought, surprised. He's really getting into the part.

Jay completed his reading without blowing a single word.

"Hey, you were great," Billy told him.

"I guess it went okay," Jay replied, smoothing back his brown hair. "I just wish I could do that well with girls."

"You seem to be doing okay with April."

Another lopsided grin. "Is she here yet?"

"Haven't seen her," Billy reported.

Jay nodded. "I hope she comes to tryouts tonight."

"Relax," Billy said. "This whole thing was her idea."

"Hi, Billy."

Billy turned to find Kylie standing next to him. She gazed at him with a smile. "I guess I'm a few minutes late."

"They just started. This will be going on for hours," Billy told her.

"Which part are you trying out for?" Kylie asked. She moved closer to him. He could smell her perfume.

"Just a little part. A delivery boy. He has five lines."

"I'm trying out for the lady vampire," Kylie informed him proudly. "I think I'm going to get it. I'm a natural."

"Is April here?" Jay asked eagerly.

Kylie frowned. "I didn't see her yet tonight," she answered.

"Was she at her house?" Jay pressed.

"Looking for me?" a voice called.

Billy turned, startled. April and Irene stood right behind them. I didn't even hear them come up, he thought.

Jay grinned. "Yeah, I thought you changed your mind," he told April.

"Not a chance," she replied. "Let's sit down." She dragged Jay to a seat in the auditorium.

Irene hurried over to sit with Nate.

"Looks like it's you and me," Kylie told him. She tossed her long hair over her shoulder and grinned.

Billy glanced at her. "I guess," he said. He wasn't sure he wanted to be stuck with Kylie. She seemed way too intense. But it wasn't as bad as he expected—Kylie seemed really into the auditions. She barely spoke to Billy as they watched all the kids read.

"Time for the part of Natalie," Ms. Aaronson finally announced, consulting her clipboard. "Let's see, who's first? Ah, Kylie. You here, Kylie?"

"Yes," Kylie replied, stepping forward.

"Do you have a last name, dear?" Ms. Aaronson asked.

"Yes," Kylie answered. "But I never use it."

Ms. Aaronson frowned, apparently trying to decide whether she should insist on having Kylie's last name. She sighed. "Okay, Kylie with no last name, you're up."

Kylie glided to the center of the stage, smiling, looking pleased with herself. Wow, Billy thought, she really likes being the center of attention.

"It's so hard being a vampire," Kylie began. "No one appreciates what we have to go through." She moaned about how much she needed human blood.

"Pretty good," said a girl's voice next to Billy. "But she's overacting a little."

Billy couldn't help laughing. "Don't tell her that!" he said. He turned to see a pretty black-haired girl standing next to him.

She smiled at him. "I shouldn't be mean. I'm probably just nervous," she admitted. "I want the same part!"

"Mae-Linn Walsh! You're up!" called Ms. Aaronson.

"Wish me luck," whispered the black-haired girl. She ran lightly up the steps to the stage.

Wow, she's really cute, Billy thought.

When she began to read, the auditorium fell silent. Mae-Linn paced back and forth, playing the part of someone faced with a major decision. She wrinkled her nose, cocked her head, smiled, frowned. Everyone watched.

I know who's going to be the star of this play, Billy decided.

Mae-Linn finished her reading. She blushed when the kids began to applaud. Then she climbed down from the stage and walked over to Billy. "You were great," he told her.

"You really think I did okay?" she asked. "I hope I get the part. It would be fun."

He studied her sparkling brown eyes. She had such soft, old-fashioned looks.

Billy felt his heart begin to beat faster.

"You doing anything after the tryouts?" she asked.

"Not really," Billy replied.

"Want to get a Coke or something?"

"Hey, great. I'd love to."

"I came with two other girls," Mae-Linn told him. "I've got to let them know." She disappeared through the curtains at the back of the stage.

This summer is looking better already, Billy decided.

Shifting his gaze toward the seats, he spotted Jay and April leaving together.

"Ms. Aaronson is supposed to announce who got the parts in a few minutes," Kylie said, coming up behind him.

"Think you'll get the lead?" Billy asked.

"Why? Do you think someone else did better than me?" Her expression darkened. Her green eyes narrowed.

"Uh, no," Billy answered, a little surprised by her reaction. "I was only asking how you thought it went."

"I got the part," Kylie assured him. "No problem."

"Well, congratulations." He wondered whether that was the right thing to say. "You were really excellent," he added.

"Want to take a walk around town, see what's happening?" she asked brightly.

"I can't."

"Why not?" Kylie demanded.

Her eyes met his. They seemed to grab him, pull him into another place. A strange, dreamlike place. He felt as though he were falling.

He forced himself to look away.

Kylie seemed surprised. And annoyed. "Why don't you want to hang out with me?" she demanded.

"I, uh, . . . I already told Mae-Linn I'd take her for a Coke."

Disappointment spread across Kylie's face.

"I'm—I'm sorry," he stammered, surprised at how upset she seemed.

Kylie turned and stalked off the stage.

"May I have your attention," Ms. Aaronson called. "Here are the names of the people I've selected for the play. Now, I want you to understand that everyone did a wonderful job. But there are only so many parts to go around . . ."

Nate, Jay, and Billy all got parts. So did April,

Kylie, and Irene. Billy wasn't surprised when Mae-Linn got the lead role.

But he saw that Kylie looked astonished.

"Hey, we both got parts," Mae-Linn called happily as she ran up to Billy.

"There was never any doubt about you," Billy replied.

"You really think so?" Mae-Linn asked shyly.

"You kidding?" Billy replied. "You were amazing."

She flashed him a dazzling smile. "Ready for that Coke?" she asked.

"Let's go," Billy answered.

He pushed open the theater door and gestured for Mae-Linn to walk ahead of him. As Billy followed her, he heard a strange sound.

A hissing sound.

Behind him.

The hiss of a snake?

"Look out!" he cried.

Chapter 6

NATE'S LUCKY SUMMER

Billy spun around, his heart pounding.

The angry hiss had sounded so close.

But he saw no snake on the ground.

Who was that, standing in the theater doorway?

He squinted into the light that flooded out from the theater. Was it Kylie?

Yes, Kylie. Standing there, so still.

Why was she *staring* at him like that?

Mae-Linn gazed up at Billy.

She looks really cute in the moonlight, he thought.

They drifted along the beach, not really going anywhere. Off to their right, waves crashed against the stone jetty.

"Is that your friend?" Mae-Linn asked.

Billy spotted a couple ahead of them on the beach. He recognized Jay and April, walking barefoot, letting the waves roll over their feet.

The moon disappeared behind a cloud, and April and Jay faded into the darkness. When the cloud passed, Jay and April had vanished.

Wow, Billy thought. Fast worker!

Mae-Linn slipped her hand into his.

I'm not doing too bad myself, Billy decided. They walked in silence for a few minutes.

"I think it's pretty late," Mae-Linn declared. "Do you know what time it is?"

Billy tried to focus on his watch, but it was too dark to see. "I can't tell," he replied.

"I'd better get back to the condo, or my parents will be worried."

"Are you doing anything tomorrow?" he asked. "Do you want to do anything? With me, I mean?"

Mae-Linn giggled at his awkwardness. "Okay," she replied brightly.

"I'll walk you home," he told her.

"Oh, don't bother," she protested. "I live right over there. I'll see you tomorrow."

She spun a complete circle, her shiny dark hair swinging out behind her. Then she dashed away, disappearing into the darkness.

It is going to be a great summer, Billy decided. A really great summer.

You didn't come here to have a great summer, he scolded himself. Remember the real reason you're here.

Billy took a deep breath and thought about Joelle. He would never forget her pale face on the sand. Never forget the two red marks on her white throat.

I will *never* forget what the vampires did to her, he swore.

Never.

He gazed down the beach. He wouldn't forget why he was here.

But Mae-Linn was certainly an added attraction.

"This is going to be a fun summer," Irene murmured, between the kisses she was giving Nate.

Fun for me, she thought. Not so much fun for you.

They sat on the porch swing in front of Nate's parents' beach condo. Irene kissed him again. The swing rocked gently. Back and forth. Back and forth.

I don't even have to cloud his mind, Irene thought. He's mine. All mine.

"It will definitely be fun," Nate agreed eagerly. "This is going to be the best summer of my life."

"I think so too," Irene whispered in his ear. "This will be a very special summer for both of us."

He studied her in the moonlight, a gigantic smile on his face.

Such a happy guy, Irene observed. He thinks he lucked out and found the girl of his dreams.

She kissed him gently on the neck.

Then slid her fangs down.

She prepared to sink them into his throat.

The need surged through her.

Hungry, she thought. So very, very hungry.

And now for a sip.

But only a sip. Don't get greedy, she warned herself. A sip. That's all.

Her fangs touched the softness of Nate's neck.

I can taste the nectar, she thought.

Taste it. Taste it. . . .

Chapter 7

BURIED TREASURE

Irene's fangs brushed Nate's throat.

A shriek exploded in her ear.

Irene jerked away from him, quickly closing her lips over the fangs.

She heard a giggle from behind the swing. Irene twisted around—and found Nate's little sister, Lynette.

Did the brat see my fangs? Irene thought. Did I hide them quickly enough?

"Lynette, what's your problem?" Nate demanded angrily.

"I gotcha!" Lynette cried happily.

Rage bubbled up inside Irene. She wanted to grab the little girl and drink her dry in one gulp.

But she had to stay calm.

She couldn't reveal herself. Couldn't upset Nate.

And couldn't lose the bet with Kylie and April.

But I was so close, she thought. So close to the nectar. She stared hungrily at Nate. If she stayed for one more minute she would lose control. She would kill Nate and his sister.

With a groan, Irene stood up. She muttered a quick goodnight, and hurried off into the darkness.

At least I don't think the little sister saw my fangs, Irene thought.

Behind her, she could hear Nate angrily scolding Lynette: "Thanks for chasing Irene away. You're dead meat!"

Thump! Thump! Thump!

Billy wandered through the dungeons of a big castle. The place was filthy. Empty and damp. Moisture glistened on the gray stone walls.

Thump-thump-thump-thump!

The noise came from above him. Someone was up there!

No one will stop me, Billy thought. No one will keep me from my revenge. Slipping the wooden stake from his bag, he started up the stone steps that led to the next level.

He reached the first landing—and stopped. An

iron gate blocked his way. He tugged on it. Securely locked.

He spotted a door hidden in the shadows. Stained, splintery wood with rusty iron hinges. He pulled on the door. It creaked as it swung open.

The room was dark and damp. Somewhere in the distance, water dripped.

Billy smiled grimly. This was exactly the kind of place they liked to sleep.

He stepped through the doorway. Spotted them instantly. Four coffins lined up against the wall.

Billy lowered his hands to the lid of the closest one. Be ready, he thought. Be ready for anything.

He slowly raised the coffin lid.

The vampire lay inside. A handsome young man with black hair. A square face.

Billy raised the wooden stake.

No hammer. Can I do it without a hammer?

Boom! Boom! Boom!

The noise again. Someone else in the castle.

Thud-thud-thud-thud!

The vampire's eyes opened. He snarled.

And lunged for Billy.

Billy jerked awake.

Bang-bang-bang-bang.

He stared around the small bedroom, breathing hard.

Someone knocking on the door. Billy shook his head, chasing away the last bits of the frightening dream. Yes. Someone was at the front door to the condo. Grabbing his robe, he stumbled to the door.

Two police officers stood on the doorstep.

"What's your name?" asked one.

"Billy."

"Your whole name."

"Billy Naughton."

"Were you out with Mae-Linn Walsh tonight?"

"Yeah," Billy replied, rubbing the last of the sleep from his eyes. "Why? What's wrong?"

"What time did you last see her?"

"Uh . . . about eleven-thirty, I guess."

"Are your parents here?"

"N-no," Billy stammered. "They only come up on weekends."

The two officers stared at him. One was a big tall guy. A walking pile of muscles. The other was a stern-looking woman. Both wore serious expressions.

"Did something happen to Mae-Linn?" Billy asked.

"She's missing," the policeman declared.

"Where did you last see her?" his partner asked.

"Uh, on the beach."

"Where on the beach?" she demanded.

"Near the edge of town. Coming from the community theater."

"Can you show us the spot?" the policeman asked.

Billy nodded.

"Get dressed and come with us."

Billy peered out from the backseat of the patrol car, watching the deserted town float by. Voices crackled over the two-way radio, but he couldn't make out what they were saying.

Mae-Linn, he thought. What happened to her? He pictured her shiny black hair, her bright smile.

Where is she?

"Slow down," he told the officers as they reached the edge of town. "It's only a little farther."

He stared at the smooth, silvery beach. "Right about here," he said. "Stop."

Billy climbed out of the patrol car. He slid down a small dune, cold sand spilling into his shoes. The police officers were right behind him, the beams from their powerful flashlights making wide yellow circles on the sand.

Billy glanced along the shoreline in both directions. "I think we walked over here."

The ocean breeze brushed back Billy's black hair. He could smell the sea. Salt air, decaying seaweed.

Mae-Linn, he thought, where did you go?

The two police officers spread out behind him, casting their lights in every direction.

Billy scanned the beach. Shadows hid within shadows.

Dangerous, he thought. The beach is dangerous at night.

A dark mound rose in front of him.

A pile of sand?

Billy started toward it. Glancing over his shoulder, he saw the beams of the police officers' flashlights. They moved down the beach, away from him.

"I found something!" he called to the police officers. He heard their footfalls as they hurried toward him.

Billy scooped away some of the sand with his hands, the cool, wet clumps spilling out between his fingers.

He touched something.

Something hard and smooth.

He brushed away the sand.

Something square.

Leather. A purse.

A purse?

"What did you find?" the policeman asked, shining his flashlight on Billy.

Billy gasped. "Mae-Linn?"

He shoveled the sand away, working frantically with both hands.

He stopped when his hand touched something cold. Cold and soft.

Billy leaned closer. Peered down.

"No—!"

He turned away. Felt his stomach lurch. And started to vomit.

Chapter 8

A SURPRISE ATTACK

Soft skin glowed white in the moonlight.

Billy recognized an arm. Mae-Linn's arm.

The officers helped to comfort Billy. Then they worked to uncover the rest of her body.

Her arms stretched out to the sides as if she were trying to make a snow angel in the sand. Strands of her shimmery dark hair covered one side of her face.

"Mae-Linn! Mae-Linn!" Billy choked out.

The officers pulled him back, away from Mae-Linn's body. "Don't touch anything," the police-woman warned.

Trembling, Billy stared at Mae-Linn. Her eyes were open, staring up at the night sky. So empty. So vacant.

Her mouth was wide open, and filled with sand. Her nostrils were filled with sand, too.

I have to know, Billy thought. I have to find out how she died.

He gazed at the police officers. They stood above Mae-Linn, speaking quietly. They weren't watching Billy.

In one quick movement, he threw himself onto the sand next to Mae-Linn. He heard the officers cry out as he reached for her shiny black hair. Pushed it away from her face. Away from her neck.

Billy studied her white throat.

In the moonlight he saw them. Two small puncture marks.

And a tiny drop of dried blood.

"No!" Billy cried, backing away from the body. "I don't believe it! Just like Joelle!"

The policeman pulled Billy back as his partner rushed to examine Mae-Linn's body. Billy barely noticed the weight of the man's hand on his arm. The two puncture marks lingered in his mind.

Vampires! The vampires did this, he thought. Mae-Linn would be alive right now if it weren't for *them!*

First Joelle, and now Mae-Linn. They have to be stopped!

I swear I'll destroy them, Billy pledged to himself once again.

I'll find them.

And I'll kill them.

Every last one of them.

Still feeling dazed, Billy sat in the cold sand. Other police officers arrived. They staked off the beach around Mae-Linn's body and strung yellow police lines around her. Finally one of them called Billy over to a cruiser.

Billy remained silent on the drive to police headquarters. The dark town whirred by as if in a dream.

The police station stood at the intersection of Main Street and Ocean Avenue. An old stone building. Bars covered the upstairs windows.

That's where the jail is, Billy thought.

He shuddered.

I'm the last one to see Mae-Linn alive, he realized. Does that make me a suspect?

Inside, a detective named Mullins grilled him, asking the same questions over and over. Where had he met Mae-Linn? When had he last seen her? Finally, about an hour before dawn, the detective let him go.

Billy walked along Main Street, passing the closed shops. No one out at that hour. Except him.

He walked faster, eager to get away from the police station, eager to get home. He wondered whether he had convinced the police of his innocence.

No way, he concluded. Detective Mullins considers me the prime suspect.

Billy thought about the barred windows on the second floor of the police station. And about Mae-Linn. And Joelle.

He shivered.

I'm going to find the vampires, he vowed. These aren't empty words. I'm going to destroy them.

He knew how to do it. He had spent a lot of time reading about vampires this past year. A lot of time preparing to kill them. He planned his revenge as he walked.

Sunlight destroys vampires. Fire does, too.

Or a wooden stake through the heart.

All I have to do is find them, Billy thought. That's the hard part.

But he knew what to look for. Vampires couldn't go out during the daylight. They couldn't eat regular food—only blood. They couldn't be seen in photographs or in mirrors.

I have all summer, Billy thought. All summer to find out which kids are vampires . . .

* * *

April stared up at the evening sky. She was annoyed.

Where are they? she wondered. Why are they always so late? I want to go into town and find the boys.

She pushed her straight blond hair out of her eyes and sighed. Kylie and Irene never seemed to hurry—no matter how hungry they were.

April pulled off her sandals. The cool sand worked its way between her toes, slid over the tops of her feet.

A whirring noise filled the air.

April watched as two bats twirled and became spinning cylinders, drawing up the beach sand and whipping it into miniature tornados.

Whirling side by side.

Dune grass thrashed the air. The wind whistled.

April shielded her eyes from the flying sand.

The whirling stopped suddenly. Sand fell back to the ground. The swaying grass became still.

Kylie and Irene stood on the beach, facing each other.

"It's about time," April snapped.

They ignored her and kept staring at each other.

"Mae-Linn went out on only one date with Billy," Irene scolded. "I can't believe you're so desperate to win our bet that you would kill her for that. You know what can happen if humans start to die."

"I *didn't* kill her," Kylie protested. "I didn't even go to the beach last night."

"Liar!" Irene replied. "You killed that girl. You're a liar, Kylie."

Kylie's eyes blazed. "Take that back," she growled.

Oh wow, April thought. These two will fight all night if I don't do something.

"The police will close the beach if we're not careful!" Irene screamed. "The food will go away! And you risked that just so you could go out with Billy and win the bet. Are you stupid or what?"

"I told you," Kylie snarled, "I didn't go near the beach."

April could feel Kylie's fury. It seemed to radiate from her, hot and intense. She took a step back.

Kylie hissed. Her fangs slid down.

Irene let out an ear-piercing screech. Her fangs lowered over her lips. Her face twisted in rage.

A chill of fear made April shudder. "Stop it!" she shrieked. "Both of you! Stop it!"

"Keep out of this!" Kylie growled.

To April's surprise, they turned on her—and attacked, snarling and hissing.

April tried to back away. But they held her tightly in place. Two pairs of fangs closed in on April's throat.

"What—what are you going to do?" she cried.

Chapter 9

ANOTHER SURPRISE ATTACK

"I have no nectar!" April cried. "You *know* I'm one of you!"

To her surprise, Irene and Kylie both tossed back their heads in laughter.

"You should've seen the look on your face, April!" Kylie declared.

"April Fools!" Irene declared. "Get it? It's April Fools' Day in June!"

They both laughed again, enjoying their joke.

April snarled and raised her long fingernails. "I'll s-s-slash you both to pieces!" she hissed furiously.

"Hey—it was just a joke," Kylie replied. "Put your claws back in. You don't have to totally lose it!"

"We're *all* losing it," Irene moaned. "Because

we're so hungry." She sighed. "Last night I was so desperate, I had to kill another dog."

Kylie and April shook their heads grimly.

Then Kylie turned to April. "Speaking of helpless creatures," she said, "how did it go with Jay last night?"

April couldn't hide her smile. "You two don't stand a chance," she replied coyly. "I'll win the bet before you even get started."

The next evening, Billy grabbed the phone as soon as he got home from work. He hadn't been able to reach Jay all day.

Jay's mom answered the phone.

"He's in his room," she told Billy. "He's been a little under the weather all day. I don't know what's wrong with him. Just a sec. I'll get him."

Billy heard the clink of the phone being put down. A few moments later, Jay came on the line.

"Hi. You hear about Mae-Linn?" Jay asked.

"Yeah, I heard." I didn't just *hear,* Billy thought. I saw her, too. "She was okay when we said goodnight on the beach. That's the last time I saw her. The police questioned me for hours. Like I'm some kind of killer. It was unreal."

"It's so weird," Jay said. "I mean, she was alive last night. And now . . ."

Jay's words trailed off. They both fell silent.

Billy wondered whether he should tell Jay about the bite marks on Mae-Linn's neck. Would his friend believe him?

"Uh—your mom says you're sick or something," Billy said.

"Yeah, I've been tired all day," Jay replied. "*Really* tired. Like I haven't slept for a week and a half."

"You sick?"

"I don't know. I'm just wrecked. And weak. Like I can't even move."

Billy drew in a breath. "Hope it isn't the flu. Are you going to make it to play rehearsal?"

"I'll try to get there. I want to see April again."

"You two got a thing going?"

"Maybe," Jay replied. "Sort of, I guess. I hope."

"Then I'll see you at the theater," Billy said. He hung up and stared out the window. I don't like this, he thought. No way do I like this. It sounds too familiar.

Joelle had always been tired last summer. Really tired. It got worse and worse as the summer went on. She walked around like a zombie. Pale. Dazed. Lost.

Until the vampire got greedy and drank too much.

And killed her.

Billy sighed. Maybe Joelle had been lucky. If

she hadn't died, she would have become one of them. Death had to be better than that.

Abruptly he slammed his fist down on the table. "I won't let them have Jay," he growled through clenched teeth. "I won't let them kill another friend."

He paced up and down the room. If he was right, if a vampire was sipping Jay's blood, the vampire had to be someone close to Jay, close enough to bite his neck.

April.

Billy tried to picture April. Her long blond hair. Her pale skin. I'll watch April, he thought. I'll look for the signs. And if she's a vampire, I'll do what I came here to do.

I'll destroy her.

Billy grabbed his script and banged out the door. He decided to stop by Nate's place on the way to the theater. If Nate was still there, they could walk to play rehearsal together.

Really dark tonight, Billy thought. Clouds filled the night sky, blocking out the moon and stars. Shadows seemed to seep out of the spaces between cottages.

Spooky, he thought. A good night for vampires to hunt.

He was glad when he reached Nate's place.

The condo was a new two-story brick building that looked as if it had been put in Sandy Hollow by mistake. Everything else in town was wood or stone. Nate's condo building didn't look as if it belonged on a beach at all!

The condo had a little park out front, with trees, a couple of swings, and a love seat. It was so dark Billy could hardly tell where he was going.

A loud snapping sound came from the trees.

Billy stopped. Listened. Silence now.

But he had heard something. Like a person hiding in the trees. Or a vampire.

Billy started for the condo, then hesitated. Someone . . . some*thing* was here. Watching him. He was sure of it. He could *feel* it.

Vampires.

Could they know why I'm here? Do they realize someone is hunting them? Will they try to kill me before I kill them?

He heard the snapping sound again. Billy whirled to face it. Nothing in the trees. Only darkness.

It's nothing, he told himself. Your imagination, that's all.

Black shadows lurked along the side of the condo. As he passed the spot where the darkness seemed deepest, he heard a scrape. Like a foot moving. Only a few feet away.

"It's nothing," Billy whispered.

Nothing.

He kept moving, eager to get to Nate's front door.

Another noise.

Scratching.

Like claws.

Tiny claws. Like a bat's claws.

An animal, Billy decided. An ordinary animal. A dog or a cat. A raccoon. Just an animal . . .

He cried out when it jumped him from behind.

Hands slid over his shoulders.

Closed on his neck.

Billy whirled to defend himself.

He saw the black shape.

Terrified, he cried out again.

Chapter 10

REHEARSAL FOR DEATH

Billy threw his hands up to defend himself. He fell back a step.

And heard laughter in the darkness.

"Got you!" Lynette squealed happily.

Billy let out a long breath. "Wow," he murmured. "I guess you did." Would his heart ever stop racing?

"Bet you thought I was one of those vampires!"

Lynette's face was barely visible in the shadows, a dim outline. But Billy knew she was grinning at him.

"You shouldn't scare people like that," Billy told her, still feeling shaky.

"Why not?"

"Because it isn't funny," Billy told her, heading for Nate's door.

"I think it's funny," Lynette insisted. "I think it's a riot!"

Billy rang the bell. A few seconds later Nate opened the door.

"Hey, man. Your little sister is evil," Billy declared.

Billy and Nate were quiet as they made their way toward the theater. It's the first rehearsal, Billy thought. The first rehearsal, and already the star is dead.

And what about Jay?

Billy recalled how pale Joelle had looked last year. How she had been weak and tired all the time.

Would the same thing happen to Jay?

The theater stood on a small grassy rise at the south edge of Sandy Hollow. A rectangular wooden building, white with green shutters and trim.

Billy could feel the fear hanging over everybody as soon as he and Nate stepped inside. All the kids had gathered on the stage. They talked in low tones about Mae-Linn.

Are any of them vampires? Billy wondered. He looked around for April, but didn't see her.

"There's Irene," Nate told him. "I'll catch you later."

Irene stood with some other girls near the steps leading down from the stage. She smiled as Nate rushed over to her.

Billy turned away from them, scanning the crowd for Jay. He drifted toward the other side of the theater.

"Someone in Sandy Hollow killed her," a brown-haired girl declared as Billy moved past her. "Maybe even someone we know."

"Hey, you hear if they're going to cancel the play?" a freckle-faced boy asked Billy.

Billy shook his head. He studied the boy. Such pale skin. Vampires didn't have tans—not even at Sandy Hollow. Other kids went to the beach every day, but not the vampires. Could this boy be a vampire?

The freckle-faced kid moved away from Billy, glancing nervously over his shoulder.

Got to remember him, Billy thought.

The theater door opened. Billy turned to see Jay walk slowly into the auditorium.

Billy's heart sank. Oh, no, he thought. Jay looks really bad.

Jay moved like a sleepwalker. Staring at the floor, he shuffled toward the stage.

Billy started across the crowded room to his best friend. But April appeared before he could get there. She took Jay's hand and pulled him down into one of the seats, talking to him, giggling at something he said.

Billy stared hard at April. Is she a vampire? Billy wondered. Is she turning my best friend into a monster?

I have to check Jay's neck for bite marks, Billy decided. Then I'll know for sure.

Someone grabbed his arm. "Hi, Billy."

Kylie stood next to him. She wore denim cutoffs and a blue halter top. Her long hair was pulled into a ponytail that hung to the center of her back. Billy stared at her. She's really beautiful, he thought. A little weird, but definitely beautiful.

"I guess you heard what happened," Kylie said quietly.

Billy nodded.

"Isn't it awful? I'm surprised so many kids came to rehearsal tonight. I thought they might be afraid to leave their houses."

"You came," Billy pointed out.

Kylie grinned. "Well, nothing scares me."

Ms. Aaronson stepped to the center of the stage and raised her hand for silence. "Let me have your attention, please."

Everyone stopped talking.

Ms. Aaronson announced that the play would go on—and that the performance would be dedicated to Mae-Linn. "Kylie will be taking over the part of Natalie," she added.

Kylie smiled brightly. "Now I get to do a scene with *you,*" she told Billy.

Billy didn't answer. He glanced around the theater, searching for Jay and April. They were nowhere to be seen. That's weird, Billy thought. Why would they leave at the beginning of rehearsal?

"Let's go. Act One," Ms. Aaronson called. "Places!"

Kylie took Billy's hand. "That's us," she told him.

He followed her to the stage, still thinking about Jay.

"All right," Ms. Aaronson said. "Begin from the beginning."

Billy moved slowly across the stage, eyeing the buildings painted on the backdrop. "Twenty-seven Bracker Street," he said. "Why can't I find it? Mr. Corkley will have my hide if I don't find it."

Billy carried a box of groceries. He was supposed to be a delivery boy trying to deliver an order. A *lost* delivery boy.

Kylie sprang out of the shadows. Acting startled, Billy nearly dropped the box of groceries.

"Looking for something?" Kylie asked with an evil smile.

"Uh . . . uh . . ." Billy stammered.

"Speak up! Are you lost?"

"I—I'm looking for 27 Bracker Street. Do you know where it is?" Billy asked.

"Right over here. I'll show you," Kylie said.

Billy followed her to stage right. His heart pounded in his chest. Why am I so nervous? he wondered. It's just a play.

But the danger seemed real. I'm good at pretending to be afraid of vampires, Billy thought. Because I *am* afraid.

Suddenly Kylie turned. Billy jumped—and dropped the groceries.

He flung up his hands. Kylie grabbed him with surprising strength.

Sharp white fangs appeared in her mouth. Her eyes glinted in the stage lights.

She pulled Billy to her and lowered her fangs to his neck.

"No!" Billy yelled. "Stop!"

He struggled to get out of Kylie's grasp.

"Not so hard!" he cried. "Hey—not so hard!"

But she buried her fangs in his throat.

Chapter 11

BIG SURPRISE FOR APRIL

"Hey! Let go!" Billy cried. "Not so hard!"

Kylie backed away. She pulled out her plastic fangs.

Billy touched the spot where Kylie bit him. No blood. The skin wasn't broken.

"I'm sorry," Kylie said. "I guess I was really getting into my part."

Billy rubbed his sore neck. Get a grip, he told himself. How will you deal with *real* vampires if you can't stay calm in a dumb play?

"Sorry I freaked," Billy told Kylie. "You really startled me. You're a good actress."

Kylie's eyes lit up. "Thanks, Billy."

"Okay. Good job," called Ms. Aaronson. "Next scene!"

Billy watched as Jay shuffled onstage. He remembered how smooth Jay had been in auditions. Today he seemed like a different person. He struggled through his lines without any energy.

"Jay is totally wiped," Billy whispered to Kylie.

"I'll say," Kylie replied. "Maybe he and April have been staying up late," she added with a smirk.

That's what I'm afraid of, Billy thought.

After rehearsal, Nate and Irene wandered over to Billy and Kylie. "Want to hang out?" Nate asked.

Before Billy could respond, Jay and April joined them. "Um, yeah!" Billy said quickly. "Why don't we *all* go down to Swanny's arcade?"

"You look as if you haven't slept in weeks," Kylie told Jay as they moved toward the theater exit.

"Just the opposite," Jay explained. "I slept all day, and then when I got up, I still felt tired."

Just like Joelle, Billy thought.

He studied Jay's neck. No bite marks. Unless they were hidden by the collar of his polo shirt.

Am I wrong about April? Billy wondered. Could Jay simply be sick?

April seemed nice enough. She and Jay held hands as they walked. So did Irene and Nate, Billy noticed.

"Hey!" called a loud voice. A tall boy wearing a maroon baseball cap stood in front of them, blocking the door to the theater. Surprised, Billy stopped.

The boy lifted his finger. Pointed.

At April, Billy realized.

He saw the color drain from April's cheeks. Her eyes went wide in alarm.

April took a step back. For a moment Billy thought she might scream.

The tall boy stared hard at April. "Hey—I remember you!" he said.

Chapter 12

BATS

What's going on? Billy wondered. Why is April so freaked out?

"Don't you remember me?" the boy asked her.

"I . . . uh . . ." April stammered.

"Rick Tyler," the boy announced. "From Shadyside."

"Oh, yeah," April replied. Taking his arm, she quickly pulled him away from Billy and the others.

"This is an old friend," she called back to them, hurrying Rick out the door. "I need to talk to him alone. Catch you guys later."

She and Rick vanished out the door.

"What was *that* about?" Irene asked.

"Beats me," Kylie replied.

"Should we wait for her?" Jay asked.

"I don't see her anywhere," Nate reported, stepping outside. "Looks like April found somebody new, Jay. Tough break, man."

Jay nodded sleepily, as if he couldn't find the strength to answer.

"Let's go," Nate urged.

They started into town. Halfway to the arcade, Jay stopped. "I can't go," he announced. "I've got to get some sleep. I can't even move."

"No way!" Billy protested. "Come on, Jay. Stay with us."

Until I figure out some way to see your neck, he thought.

"Can't," Jay mumbled. He trudged slowly away toward the beach—and his condo.

Billy rushed after Jay, the loose sand feeling spongy under his sandals. He caught up with Jay on the other side of the dunes.

"Wait up," he called.

Jay stopped. "What?"

"Let me see your neck." Billy reached for Jay's collar.

"Hey—" Jay protested, knocking Billy's hand away.

"I need to see your neck," Billy insisted.

Jay frowned. "Are you crazy? What is your *problem?*"

"I think you've been bitten by a vampire."

Jay stared at him for a long moment. Then he

gave a short laugh. "Billy, go away. I'm too beat to listen to this."

Billy reached for Jay's collar again.

"No way!" Jay shouted, pushing Billy away.

Billy stumbled back, nearly losing his balance. I didn't think Jay had enough strength left to do that, he thought.

"I don't want to hear this vampire stuff!" Jay cried. "I'm too tired."

What should I do? Billy wondered. Should I tackle him? Rip off his shirt?

"Billy, I don't know how to say this," Jay started. "But you were in a mental hospital. And now you're acting crazy. I mean, I'm worried about you. Are you sure you're okay?"

"You think I'm crazy," Billy muttered.

"You're talking about *vampires!*" Jay exclaimed.

"Jay, you have to listen to me—" he began.

But a voice interrupted him. "Hey, Billy! You coming?" Kylie stood on the crest of the dune with Nate and Irene, watching them.

Billy hesitated.

"Go on, man," Jay told him. "Stop thinking about your old girlfriend. There's no such thing as a vampire."

Billy glared at his best friend. But he couldn't force Jay to show him his neck. Not with the others watching. They would *all* think he'd gone nuts.

He walked back toward Kylie.

Jay will be okay for tonight, he told himself. He's too wiped to do anything but go straight home. And April is with that Rick guy.

By the time they reached the center of town, Nate and Irene had disappeared.

"Hey, where did they go?" Billy asked Kylie.

"Don't know," Kylie answered. "Maybe they wanted to be alone."

"I guess," Billy replied.

Their eyes met. Billy started to look away, but her gaze held him. Her eyes seemed to glow softly, pulling him in. Gently. Slowly.

Billy felt a weird tug in his chest.

He felt as if he were floating.

Gliding in a mist.

Alone with Kylie. Beautiful Kylie.

Drifting past the Mini Market.

The Pizza Cove.

The Harbor Palace movie theater.

Billy shook the weird dreaminess off. Kylie stared at him, frowning, her green eyes smoldering.

They stood in front of the Old Atlantic Chowder House, people pushing past them to get in and out. How did we get here? Billy wondered. Kylie's eyes still burned into his.

"Uh . . . want some chowder?" he asked awkwardly.

Kylie shrugged. "Sure. Why not?"

The place had fishing nets on the walls and red-checked plastic tablecloths. Waiters hurried past with steaming bowls of chowder, the tangy aroma drifting through the room.

"The menu is over there," Billy told Kylie, pointing to a large blackboard on a stand. The day's offerings were scribbled in chalk.

Kylie studied the menu, then shrugged. "I guess I'm not really hungry." She laughed. "I never eat. I never seem to have the time."

"We don't have to eat if you don't want to," Billy told her.

They left the restaurant.

"Come on," Kylie urged, grabbing his hand. "Let's check out the beach."

Billy wasn't sure he wanted to return to the beach so soon. He thought of Mae-Linn. He pictured her body again, half covered with sand. It was hard to shake such an ugly memory.

But Kylie *was* really hot.

He decided to follow her. As they crossed Main Street, he searched for April and Rick Tyler, or Irene and Nate. No sign of them.

Kylie chose a spot where they had to climb down to the beach through the dune grass. It clung to Billy's ankles as if the blades were covered with sticky glue.

The moon shone brightly in the star-filled sky, bathing the beach in silvery light. Billy stopped to scrape some beach tar from his sandals.

Kylie seemed distracted, distant. Billy thought she had a strange expression on her face. Needy? Longing?

"Let's sit down," she suggested.

"I want to keep walking," Billy told her.

Kylie's eyes flashed angrily. Then she smiled. Slipped her hand into Billy's.

What's her deal? Billy wondered.

They walked along the beach holding hands. Kylie gazed at him. "You're sort of . . . well, hard to get to know," she told him. "You never talk about yourself."

"I don't like to talk about myself," he replied.

"Well, we don't have to talk," Kylie murmured, moving closer to him. She tilted her face to his. Billy stared into her eyes. Felt himself falling . . . falling into Kylie's eyes.

Drifting.

Everything looks blurry, he thought. Can't see anything.

Only Kylie. He heard her whispering his name, pulling him down to the sand.

A loud flapping sound shook Billy from his

daze. Something fluttered past his nose, so close he could feel the breeze from its wings.

Startled, Billy looked up. Something black flashed past his head. A dark shadow in the moonlight.

Something slammed against his shoulder.

He ducked out of the way as tiny claws grazed his cheek.

Bats?

Yes, two of them.

They swooped down again, one clawing at his shoulder, the other going for his face. He ducked out of the way.

Desperately searching the beach, he tried to find some cover. A dock to hide beneath. An abandoned beach umbrella.

Something. Anything. But there was nowhere to hide.

He glanced up, searching for the bats. They flew over him.

Circling.

Hissing.

Then they swooped to attack.

Chapter 13

VAMPIRE ISLAND

Billy hit the sand. He scrambled to his knees and tried to roll away.

The bats uttered shrill shrieks as they attacked.

As Billy tried to roll away, he saw Kylie leap to her feet. She swung her hands wildly, thrashing the air.

She hit one bat. The sound of her hand hitting its plump body made a loud *thock.*

The bats stopped their ugly screeching.

The other one hovered over Kylie. She swung again, narrowly missing it.

She let out a loud victory cry as the bats rose up, then swooped away.

Billy sat up in the sand. "Wow," he murmured. "Wow. You were great!"

"I'm not afraid of bats," Kylie boasted.

"I'm not either—unless they attack me," Billy said. He felt embarrassed that Kylie had to fight while he rolled helplessly in the sand.

"There are so many bats on this beach," he said. "They all live on that island out there."

"Know what I'd like to do?" Kylie asked excitedly. "Row out to the island and explore! Want to?"

Billy stared at her in surprise. "You mean right now? Wouldn't it be better to go in the daytime?"

"No," Kylie replied, tugging on his arm. "Come on. Let's do it now. It will be cool."

"Well . . ." Billy hesitated. He didn't really want to go. But he didn't want to look any more like a total wimp.

"We need a boat," Kylie said.

"The guy I work for has some rowboats," Billy told her. "He said I can borrow them whenever I want. I guess we could get one and go out there now."

"Where are the rowboats?"

"Down by the wharf. Come on. I'll show you."

They started jogging down the beach.

"Hey, there's Irene and Nate!" Kylie exclaimed.

Billy spotted them walking close together. I guess they *did* want to be alone, he thought.

"I've got to tell her where we're going," Kylie said. "She'll be so jealous!"

"I'll get a boat while you talk to her," Billy offered. "I'll pick you up at that long dock—the one everybody dives from."

"See you there," Kylie agreed. "I can't wait."

Billy let the rowboat glide slowly up to the long dock. No sign of Kylie.

Where is she? he wondered. Maybe she changed her mind.

He tied the boat to a cleat and jumped onto the dock, scanning the beach. Still no Kylie. He didn't see Nate or Irene, either.

Billy climbed back into the little boat. Waited.

"Hey!" Kylie's sandals thumped on the wooden planks as she hurried down the dock. "Ready?"

"What took you so long?" he demanded.

Kylie shrugged. "Sorry," she said absently. "You ready to explore the island?"

Billy felt the boat rocking beneath him, making small waves against the dock. "Let's go," he told her. Slipping the oars into the oarlocks, he propelled the boat away from the dock and aimed it at the island.

The vampire island.

Nighttime, he thought. They will be awake.

But they won't be home, Billy told himself. Night is when they have to feed, and there's no food on the island. They go to Sandy Hollow for food. For *human* food.

"The island isn't very far," Kylie commented. "It shouldn't take long."

Billy rowed, the oarlocks creaking and groaning.

Kylie sat in the stern, grinning excitedly at him, her eyes flashing. "I love to do things like this," she told him. "Weird, crazy things. Just because I feel like it."

Billy saw bats flying over the water. Bats swooped low over the boat. They rose to become black shadows in the star-filled sky. They circled and swooped in again, passing only a few feet over Billy's head.

"It's almost like they're warning us off," Billy declared.

"Yeah. Right." Kylie rolled her eyes. "Don't worry," she said. "The bats won't hurt you. Bats are good. Didn't you learn that in school?"

Billy glanced over his shoulder and caught sight of the island. A long, low shape against the dark sky. Waiting.

Waiting for me, Billy thought.

The island stood black against the blue-black water.

Not a single light anywhere.

Am I totally crazy? Billy wondered as he gazed at the vampire island.

Am I going to regret this?

PART TWO

BILLY'S QUEST

Chapter 14

A SURPRISE WELCOME

"There!" Kylie exclaimed, pointing to an old dock, bobbing in the water. "We can tie the boat to that dock."

As Billy guided the boat toward it, he studied the island. Darkness hid everything beyond the end of the dock. Tall trees towered over the shoreline, blocking out the moon, making the night even darker.

"This place is too weird," Billy muttered.

Bats flapped overhead. The sky was full of them. They fluttered from tree to tree. From the dock into the darkness. Billy heard a low growl carried on the wind. Were there dogs on the island, too? If so, they had to be wild. Another howl made him shiver.

"Isn't this exciting?" Kylie asked breathlessly.

Only if you have a death wish, Billy thought.

He eased the rowboat up to the dock. Kylie tied it to a ladder.

"Come on," she urged. "This is so cool. Let's see what's here." She started up the ladder.

"Watch out," Billy cautioned. "Half the rungs are missing."

Kylie made it easily to the top. "Come on up," she urged him. "It held me okay."

The rung Billy grabbed was covered with some sort of slimy, dark goo. He reached down to rinse his hand in the water.

Something instantly splashed to the surface. Startled, he yanked his hand out of the murky water.

"It was just a fish!" Kylie exclaimed, laughing.

Billy took a deep breath, then climbed the ladder.

"Let's go!" Kylie urged.

They moved slowly onto the island, stepping cautiously in the darkness.

A shrill cry made Billy jump.

"What was that?" he gasped.

"Probably a bird or something," Kylie replied. "I bet there are all kinds of things living here." She glanced over her shoulder at Billy. "They're probably all harmless," she added.

Nothing here is harmless, Billy thought. Some

of the creatures on this island are very dangerous.

They killed Joelle.

Vines and bushes clogged the path leading inland from the dock. The plants felt slimy and cold as he pushed through.

Billy searched for the burned-out houses. But he didn't see any houses at all. Maybe that was only a story.

Maybe everything he's heard about the island was a lie. Stories told again and again. Stories that grew wilder each time they were repeated, until there was no truth left in them.

No way, Billy thought. He knew one story about this island was true. A horror story. About vampires.

"I see something up ahead," Kylie whispered. She crashed through the bushes and disappeared from sight.

Billy followed her. Kylie led the way up to a tall, dark ruin. The remains of a burned house.

Most of it had collapsed, but jagged boards remained standing. Dark and charred.

"We should have brought flashlights," Billy commented.

"It's more fun this way," Kylie insisted. Her eyes met his. "Are you scared?" she teased.

Before Billy could answer, he heard a low moan.

From the trees around the house.

He turned back to the woods. But saw only shadows.

Ignore it, he told himself. It's just an animal.

Kylie had already started down an overgrown path. Billy went after her. The path led to another burned-out house. This one was still a shell, gutted by fire.

Billy examined the door. Only a small piece of it remained. A charred chunk of wood attached by a single hinge. Blackness oozed from the doorway.

Kylie stuck her head inside. "Look," she breathed.

Billy peered into the house—and gasped.

Bats.

Everywhere.

Hanging from the ceiling.

The doorways.

A few clung to the overhead light fixtures.

Two of them detached themselves from the ceiling—and launched themselves at Billy and Kylie. Billy raised his hand to protect his face. But the bats flapped past him and vanished.

He clung to the door frame, his heart racing.

This is the vampire island, he thought. Every one of these bats could be a vampire. Any one of them could attack us. Kill us.

His gaze fell on a charred piece of wood. It looked like it had once been a table leg.

Billy reached down and grabbed it. The wood felt heavy in his hand.

"Let's get out of here," Kylie suggested. She pushed past him and continued down the path. Billy followed.

A long, loud howl made Billy stop. He searched the trees frantically.

Kylie had disappeared.

Another howl. Closer this time.

"Kylie!" Billy yelled. Where was she? Why didn't she answer? "Kylie, get back here!"

Silence.

Billy held his breath as he peered into the trees. No sign of Kylie.

No animal. Nothing there.

Then—branches snapped. Dry leaves crackled.

Footsteps.

An animal charging through the trees.

Billy spun to face the sound.

Too late. A snarling black creature sprang at him. Knocked him to the ground.

Its yellow eyes glowed as it sank razor-sharp fangs into Billy's neck.

Chapter 15

NOT A REGULAR WOLF

Billy rolled to the side as the creature fell on him. Its teeth grazed his neck, catching in his hair. He felt its hot, sour breath on his face.

Billy gagged. He couldn't breathe.

Yellow eyes stared down at him. He shoved the creature away with both hands.

What *is* it? he wondered. Is it a wolf?

The creature attacked again.

Billy held the charred table leg in front of his face. The creature's fangs sank into the wood.

With a yelp it fell back, shaking the stick from its mouth.

Billy scrambled to his feet. Yes—it's a wolf! he realized.

He dove for the wooden table leg. Grabbed it

off the ground. And spun around, holding it in front of him like a sword.

The wolf leapt again.

And Billy drove the wooden table leg deep into its chest.

The yellow eyes narrowed in pain. But the creature didn't cry out, didn't utter a sound.

Billy stared at the deep hole in the wolf's chest. No blood. It didn't bleed.

Not a regular wolf, Billy saw to his horror. *Not a regular wolf.*

Now the yellow eyes glowed with fury. The wolf twisted away, opening its jaws wide, yanking the end of the stick from Billy's hand.

Was it about to attack again?

No.

Its eyes rolled up and it crumpled onto its back on the ground. All four legs thrashed the air for a moment. Then the creature let out a long sigh—and lay still.

Billy stood over it, struggling to catch his breath. He had just killed a vampire, he realized. A vampire he had disturbed. One that decided to attack him in wolf form.

He lightly prodded the black fur with his foot. Clumps of fur fell off the body.

His heart still pounding, Billy turned away. The woods stretched silently all around.

The whole island must be filled with monsters like this, Billy realized.

"Kylie." He murmured her name out loud.

Where is Kylie? he wondered.

I've got to show her this creature. She's got to see a real vampire. She'll believe me. Then everyone will believe me about the vampires here at Sandy Hollow.

"Kylie!" He shouted her name.

"Kylie!" He cupped his hands around his mouth and called to her.

Following the path that had brought them to the burned-out house, Billy trotted into the woods. "Kylie—where are you? Kylie?"

He found her sitting on a log on a low, sandy hill overlooking the water. She turned as he ran up to her, and jumped to her feet. "Billy—what's wrong?"

"I—I couldn't find you," he cried breathlessly.

"Sorry," she said. "I thought you were right behind me. But when I turned around, you were gone." She smiled. "I knew you'd find me. I—"

She stopped, catching the alarmed expression on Billy's face. "What's wrong? You're all scratched. What happened?"

The whole story burst out of him in a flood of words. "A vampire, Kylie. In wolf form. It attacked me. Outside that burned-out house. But I drove a stake through its chest. I killed it."

He grabbed her hand and started to pull her to the house. "Come on. You have to see it. I want to prove to you there are vampires here. I want you to see with your own eyes."

"But, Billy—" She pulled back.

"Hurry, Kylie. I'm going to prove it to you."

She narrowed her eyes at him. "Did you hit your head or something? You're talking crazy. Everyone knows there are no real vampires."

"Come on. Hurry." He tugged her harder.

She rolled her eyes and groaned. But she followed him.

He led the way through the trees. The chittering of bats overhead grew louder as they neared the house. A distant howl floated eerily over the whisper of the wind.

Through the trees, Billy spotted the dark outline of the burned-out house. "Here it is!" he told her. "Right in front. You'll see, Kylie. You'll see I'm telling the truth."

He led the way out of the trees. Then he pulled her across the wet grass. "There—!" He pointed.

And then they both gasped in shock.

Chapter 16

ROMANCE

"There's nothing there!" Kylie exclaimed.

Billy bent down and examined the spot. No sign of his struggle. No sign of the vampire wolf. The grass wasn't even bent.

"It—it must have been over here," he stammered. He ran across the grass, first one way, then the other. He trotted up to the house, then back, trying to retrace his steps.

Nothing here. Not a sign.

Kylie rolled her eyes again. "Lame, Billy. Really lame," she groaned.

"You have to believe me—!" Billy cried shrilly.

"It's not a very funny joke," Kylie said. She took his arm and pressed her cheek against his shoulder. Then she spoke in a tiny voice. "Are you trying to scare me so you can be my big, brave protector?"

"No. Really—" Billy insisted.

Clinging to his arm, she rubbed her nose against his cheek. "Come back to the log," she whispered. "It's such a pretty spot."

She doesn't believe me, Billy realized. She thinks it was some kind of joke. If I keep insisting, she'll just think I'm some kind of a jerk. Or that I'm crazy.

He let her pull him back to the low hill overlooking the water. "We—we have to get back," he stammered, gazing out toward the water.

"It's early. Let's see what else there is to explore," Kylie suggested.

"No way," Billy answered. "We're going back to the boat. There's nothing here."

Nothing but vampires, he thought.

"Just sit with me for one minute," Kylie begged. "Then we'll leave, I promise. It's so beautiful here."

Billy stared at her. He wanted to leave. Wanted to run to the boat as fast as he could. But Kylie looked so beautiful sitting there, moonlight washing over her red hair.

She patted the log beside her.

Billy sat down. The bark felt damp and crumbly beneath him. The cold air pressed in around them.

When did it get so foggy? Billy wondered. He could barely see anything beyond the clearing. It seemed as if he and Kylie were alone in an island of fog.

Billy suddenly felt drowsy. A little dizzy.

Kylie moved closer to him on the log. "See? Isn't this nice?" she asked softly.

Billy tried to focus his eyes on Kylie. The pale moonlight played over her face. She was truly beautiful, he realized. Her face belonged on a fashion model—or a movie star. And the way her long red hair glowed . . .

Kylie leaned over and kissed him.

She pulled back. Gazed into his eyes, smiled, and kissed him again.

A long, slow kiss.

This is wild, Billy thought. She is really *hot!*

The kiss continued. Billy felt as if he were drifting . . . falling . . .

Bats fluttered overhead. Billy paid no attention to them.

He was drifting . . . drifting . . .

He felt Kylie's mouth move from his lips to his neck.

Chapter 17

"NOT JAY!"

Billy stood up. "I—I feel so strange," he said. "Kind of dizzy. We'd better go."

"Billy, sit down," Kylie insisted. "Billy—please."

He shook his head, trying to force away the strange dizziness.

Kylie jumped up. She stepped closer. And kissed him again.

The world seemed to be spinning. The dark trees whirled.

Billy wanted to give in to it, to let the spinning world take him, whisk him away. He wanted to stand in that moonlit clearing and kiss Kylie forever.

No.

He shook his head.

The spinning stopped.

"I've really got to get home," Billy insisted, pulling Kylie toward the boat.

Holding her hand, he pulled her through the trees. He could tell Kylie was annoyed by the way she slapped the branches out of her way, not saying anything. They passed the burned-out houses. Hurrying onto the dock, Billy climbed down the ladder, then helped Kylie into the boat.

Billy rowed toward the mainland in silence. Whenever he glanced at Kylie, anger flashed in her eyes.

She is spoiled, Billy decided. She pouts whenever she doesn't get her own way.

Bats fluttered overhead, swooping low over the tiny rowboat. A dark cloud inched its way across the face of the moon. The night grew darker and darker as Billy rowed toward the shore.

He guided the boat to the long dock and tied it up. Kylie hadn't said a word since they left the island. She seemed to be studying him.

Billy climbed onto the dock, then reached down to pull Kylie up. Her hand felt cold, as if the island's dampness had seeped into her skin. The last yellow sliver of the moon disappeared behind the black cloud as they stepped from the dock onto the beach.

Billy moved carefully, trying to see where he was going.

So dark.

"I don't know why we had to leave so early," Kylie complained, pressing her forehead against his shoulder.

"I do," Billy muttered. "That island was dangerous."

Kylie laughed. "Dangerous?"

Billy didn't want to be teased. He stomped on ahead.

"Billy—?" he heard Kylie call. Then he heard a small shriek. "Billy!" Kylie cried shrilly.

Billy spun around and ran back to Kylie. "What is it?"

"Billy, look . . ." Kylie whispered, holding her hands to her face, staring down in horror at the sand.

"Oh no!" Billy groaned.

A boy. Sprawled on his back in the sand. Staring up lifelessly at the sky. His neck twisted, twisted at such a wrong angle.

"Noooo!" Billy wailed, dropping down beside the boy. "Not Jay! Please—not Jay!"

Chapter 18

PIZZA FOR A VAMPIRE

Billy leaned over his friend—and gasped again.

"It—it *isn't* Jay!"

"I recognize him," Kylie said weakly, her hands still pressed tightly against her cheeks. "Don't you remember? He's the guy April went off with earlier tonight."

"Yes—Rick," Billy remembered.

He leaned over the body. Brushed swarming sand flies off the boy's face.

His eyes stopped at the throat.

At the two puncture wounds in the neck. A tiny drop of blood clung to each hole.

Rick's face was as white as flour.

He's been drained, Billy realized. Completely drained.

"This is so . . . awful," Kylie moaned.

"And what about April? Where is she? Do you think something has happened to her?"

Billy couldn't take his eyes off the twin red puncture marks.

No, he thought. Nothing has happened to April. Nothing has happened to that vampire.

Not yet.

The next night Billy met his friends at the Pizza Cove. Everyone was there—Nate, Jay, Irene, Kylie, and April—sitting at two tables pulled together.

"After we found Rick's body, Billy called the police from a pay phone on Main Street," Kylie explained. "I was really freaked out. I couldn't even talk. But he was great."

Yeah, great, Billy thought glumly. And I was questioned for more than an hour. It's a good thing Kylie was there to back up my story. That's the second murder I've been involved in. The second one . . .

Billy studied his friends' faces as Kylie told them about Rick Tyler. Jay seemed even more tired than last night. He sat beside April, staring at the others with bloodshot eyes.

He can hardly hold his head up, Billy thought. This is really bad news.

Billy studied Jay's neck. He didn't see any bite marks. But he was sure they were there.

Billy shifted his gaze to April. How many sips has she taken? he wondered. Three sips, and Jay becomes a vampire. How close is he?

April shredded her paper napkin, tearing off little pieces and putting them in a pile. Her hands shook.

She seems really upset, Billy thought.

But he knew she was acting.

"I can't believe I was the last person to see Rick alive," April said tearfully.

Jay offered her a slice of pizza.

"I can't eat," she declared, shaking her head. "I'm too upset."

Of course she can't eat, Billy thought. Vampires can't eat food.

He studied April's face. Her smooth white cheeks. Not a trace of a tan. She had never been out in the sun, he knew. If she saw sunlight, she would die.

Nate sighed. "You know, all I want is to have a great summer," he said. "But nobody is having fun. There are police all over the beach and the town. Everyone is so upset about the two murders. I even heard someone else say *vampires* are the killers!"

"I'm really sick of hearing about vampires," Irene declared.

"It's so stupid," Kylie agreed. "Everyone

knows there is no such thing. I can't believe people are so superstitious."

"They're real," Billy told her. He kept his eyes on April. "Don't let anybody tell you they're not."

April glanced at him, her expression blank, as if she wasn't interested in what he was saying. What a great actress, Billy thought. She should be the star of the play.

"You don't really believe that, do you?" Irene asked.

"Yes, he does," Jay chimed in. "Billy has been talking about vampires ever since we got here!"

Nate and Irene laughed.

Billy felt a hot ball of anger growing in his chest. He forced himself to stay calm. Ignore them, he told himself. Don't get into an argument about it.

Irene took Nate's arm and pulled him out of his chair. "You promised to take me dancing," she told him.

"I'm a total klutz," Nate protested.

"No problem," Irene informed him. "I'll show you everything you need to know."

Nate shrugged. "Anyone else want to come?"

They all shook their heads.

After Nate and Irene left, Billy turned his attention back to April. He studied her as she joked and flirted with Jay. She was pretty cute, with straight blond hair and beautiful emerald eyes.

She's a vampire, he reminded himself.

Not a cute girl. Not a nice girl.

A vampire.

"Have some pizza," Billy said. He shoved a slice of pizza in April's face.

She reacted with disgust.

He knew she would.

"No thanks," she said, waving it away. "I can't eat. Really."

"No. Try it," Billy insisted. He shoved it under her nose again. "It's really excellent." He wanted to make her squirm.

"No. Really," April said sharply, pulling her head back.

"Just a taste," Billy insisted.

"Give her a break, man," Jay cut in. "What's your problem, anyway?"

Billy slowly lowered the pizza slice to the plate. He kept his eyes on April.

She knows that I know, he realized.

She knows that I know the truth about her. She's probably thinking about how she can shut me up.

Billy felt a chill of fear.

I'm in danger now, he told himself. Real danger.

But not if I act first.

PART THREE

BILLY AND KYLIE

Chapter 19

VAMPIRES EVERYWHERE

The next evening, Kylie and Irene strolled on the beach.

Irene is looking really happy and excited, Kylie thought, studying her friend. *I guess she's made real progress with Nate. She probably thinks she's going to win our bet.*

Irene bent to pick up a horseshoe crab shell. She peered inside it, then tossed it back to the sand. "How is it going with Billy?" she asked.

Kylie sighed. "Billy has been a problem," she admitted. "He keeps seeing vampires everywhere."

Irene's eyes lit up. "That *is* a problem!"

Both girls laughed.

"I'm meeting Nate later at Swanny's," Irene

revealed. "I think tonight could be . . . delicious." An evil grin spread over her face.

"I came so close last night," Kylie told her. "So close I could taste the nectar. But . . ." Her voice trailed off.

"But what?" Irene demanded, brushing back her hair, letting the ocean wind flutter it.

Kylie shook her head. She frowned. "I don't want to talk about it. I'm so hungry, Irene. So hungry."

Irene started to reply. But Kylie dove to the sand.

Kylie struck quickly—and grabbed a plump sea gull off the ground. She tightened her hand around its feathery throat.

The bird flapped its wings. It let out a sharp squawk.

Its cry was cut off by Kylie's fingernails as they dug deep into its flesh and ripped out the bird's throat.

As dark blood flowed over the white feathers, Kylie buried her face in the open wound. Slurping loudly. Drinking frantically. Pressing the warm bird over her face as she drank.

"Hey—how about sharing?" Irene demanded, reaching out her hand.

Kylie hungrily drank some more. Then she dropped the gull into Irene's hand. Irene raised the bird's torn body to her face and drank.

"Save some for April," Kylie said, wiping blood off her cheeks with both hands.

"She can get her own," Irene replied, her face buried in the dead sea gull.

"Jay, hi. It's me," Billy said, balancing the phone between his shoulder and ear. He bent over and tied his sneakers as he talked.

"How's it going?" Jay asked dully.

"I've got to talk to you," Billy replied. Jay still sounds tired, he thought with alarm. I hope I'm not too late.

"Can't really talk now," Jay said, so low Billy could barely hear him. "Got to meet April. I've got to—"

"That's what I want to talk to you about," Billy interrupted. He finished tying the sneaker and sat up, grabbing the phone.

"April?" Jay asked, confused.

"Yes. Listen to me, Jay. I know it's hard to believe. But you're in danger. Real danger."

On the other end of the line, Jay let out a weak laugh.

"I'm totally serious," Billy insisted. "Don't laugh, Jay. Just listen to me."

"I'm not feeling well," Jay said, clearing his throat. "I've got to go, man. Really."

"Just listen to me!" Billy insisted. "Don't you

wonder why you're so tired? Don't you wonder why you feel so weak? It's because of April."

A long silence on Jay's end. Then, "Huh?"

"April is a vampire, Jay," Billy declared heatedly. "I know it's hard to believe. But she's a vampire. She's drinking your blood, a sip at a time. If you don't watch out—"

"Cut it out!" Jay snapped. "I told you, I'm late. I've got to go. These dumb vampire jokes—"

"It's not a joke," Billy insisted desperately. "I told you what happened last summer. It's happening again, Jay. You've got to listen. I'm trying to save your life. April will—"

"Billy, take a deep breath, man," Jay interrupted. "Listen to me. I'm feeling tired because I have the flu or something. All this vampire talk—well . . . Are your parents there?"

"Well . . . yeah," Billy replied.

"Have you talked with them about this vampire stuff?"

"No," Billy told him.

"Maybe you should," Jay urged. "Maybe you should tell them that you're troubled by thoughts about vampires. They can help you, Billy. You really should give your parents a chance to help you."

He thinks I'm crazy, Billy realized.

Here he is, in danger for his life—and he's worrying about me.

"I've got to go," Jay said. "April is here. At the condo. Maybe I'll see you later, Billy."

"No—!" Billy cried. "Don't go! Don't go with her, Jay! Please—!"

Billy heard a click. The phone went dead.

A raindrop hit Billy's cheek. The icy bead of water trickled down his neck, making his skin tingle.

The fog seemed to be thickening. It blanketed the town, turning the street lamps into misty blurs of yellow light.

Billy turned down Main Street. He searched for Jay and April in the Pizza Cove. Not there.

Billy pushed open the door of Swanny's ice-cream parlor and arcade. The damp night disappeared immediately. Loud music blared around him. Kids were laughing and talking over the music. Bent over video games.

Nate and Irene sat on a low bench near the jukebox, clinging together. Irene had her arms around Nate's shoulders. She was kissing him.

Billy walked quickly over to them. "Hey, do you guys know where Jay and April are?" he asked.

Irene turned. She had lipstick smeared over her mouth. Nate shot Billy an annoyed look. He signaled with both hands, as if to say, 'Get lost.'

"Have you seen him?" Billy demanded.

"Not since yesterday," Nate replied impatiently.

"I really need to find him," Billy said. "He's in danger."

That caught Irene's attention. She pulled away from Nate and raised her eyes to Billy. "Danger?"

"April is a vampire," Billy blurted out. "I tried to warn Jay. But he won't believe me. She's a vampire and she's—"

"Give it a rest, man," Nate said impatiently. He scowled at Billy.

"No. Really—" Billy started.

Nate narrowed his eyes menacingly. "I mean it. Give this vampire stuff a rest. You're starting to sound weird, Billy. You're starting to sound really messed up."

Nate turned back to Irene. She smiled at him and slid her hands behind his neck, pulling his face to hers.

No help there. Billy glanced around the arcade. He searched the crowd for Jay and April.

A familiar squeal of laughter caught his attention. Lynette. She was playing an old Ninja Turtles game at the back of the arcade, near the fire exit.

A lanky, older boy, dressed entirely in black, leaned over the game as Lynette played.

No! It's impossible, Billy thought, recognizing the boy immediately.

A face I'll never forget. Never.

The face of pure evil.

"Nate!" Billy cried. He grabbed Nate by the shoulder and tried to pry him away from Irene.

"Hey! Give me a break!" Nate protested angrily.

"Nate—your sister!" Billy cried. "There's a guy over there with your sister—that guy in black—"

"Oh, that's just Jon," Nate told him. "I know him from last summer. He said he'd watch Lynette if I got him an early tee time tomorrow at the golf club."

"Nate, you can't leave Lynette with that guy!" Billy shrieked. He tugged Nate's arm again. "He's a vampire, Nate. I know he is! He's a vampire! He'll—"

"Whoa! Let go!" Nate jerked his arm away. He jumped to his feet, and loomed angrily over Billy, bumping him with his powerful chest. "Back off, Billy. I mean it."

"Listen to me—" Billy wailed.

"You're messed up, man," Nate told him. "You're seeing vampires everywhere you look. Get home, Billy. Get yourself home, okay? You're really messed up."

"Maybe we should help him home," Irene suggested. "Or maybe we should get him to a doctor or something."

"Nooo!" Billy cried. "I'm telling the truth! I'm not crazy!"

He spun away from them—in time to see the tall boy pull Lynette out the fire door in back.

Chapter 20

CHEST PAINS

"No—stop!" Billy screamed.

A few kids turned from their games to stare at him.

Billy pushed his way through the crowded aisle to the fire door.

Jon is a vampire, he told himself. Jon is the vampire who murdered Joelle.

Now where is he taking Lynette?

He pushed the heavy fire door open with his shoulder, stepped outside, and let the heavy door slam behind him. The rain had stopped, but the air remained cool and wet.

He stood in a small alley behind the arcade. Where are they? he thought frantically. Where did Jon take her?

He let his eyes search up and down the alley. No vampire.

Would he really hurt a little kid? Billy thought.

"Help me!"

Lynette's cry. From nearby.

Which way? Billy wondered. He spun around. Tried to tell where the cry came from.

"Help me!" He heard it again.

He's taking her to the beach, Billy realized. The deserted beach.

Billy sprinted from the alley. The beach was a short distance away. But it seemed to take forever, even running full speed. Finally, he clambered down the wooden steps that led to the sand.

His sneakers dug into the rain-wet sand as he started to run.

"Lynette? Lynette?"

No reply.

He stopped short.

A dying fire still smoldered near the shore. Drenched by the rain. The last sparks of somebody's interrupted beach party.

And in the dim orange light of the low fire, Billy saw Lynette, sprawled on her back on the sand. Arms straight out. Head tilted at an angle. Not moving.

"Hey—!" Jon stepped forward to meet Billy. "Stay away from here!" he shouted, his voice deep and menacing over the steady rush of ocean waves behind him.

"I—I know you," Billy stammered.

The closer Jon came, the taller he appeared. His eyes flashed as he narrowed them on Billy. A dark orange flash, the same color as the dying fire.

You're dead, Billy thought. *You're dead, Jon. I killed you last summer. After you killed Joelle.*

But no.

Billy had obviously failed.

"I know you," Billy repeated. "You killed my girlfriend. You killed Joelle."

The vampire sneered. "Was that her name?"

"You—you—" Billy couldn't choke out any words.

The vampire snorted. "Bad break, kid. But that's the way it goes sometimes," he said with a smirk.

"You killed her—and you didn't even know her name," Billy managed to say.

"Sometimes I like fast food," the vampire said, snickering at his own joke. "I don't always have time for introductions."

Billy turned his gaze to the fire, thinking hard, the rage burning in his chest. "How can you joke about it?" he cried. "How can you joke about taking human lives?"

The vampire shrugged. "You're interrupting

my dinner." He motioned to Lynette, sprawled motionless on the sand. "Maybe I'll save the little girl for a late-night snack. You can be the main course." He let his fangs slide down over his lower lip.

His orange eyes flashed brightly. He began to rise up over Billy, floating off the ground.

"No—!" Billy uttered a sharp cry and dove past him.

Stumbling, sliding on the wet sand, Billy hurtled to the dying embers. A weathered piece of driftwood had just caught fire. It burned dully, purple-red flames licking up from the charred log.

Billy grabbed the burning log off the sand—and whirled around.

As Jon dove for him, Billy swung the flaming log at the vampire's chest.

"Die!" Billy screamed. "Die! Die! Die!"

But to Billy's shock, the vampire grabbed the burning log with both hands.

He tugged it easily from Billy's grasp. Held it by one end.

Billy's arms flew up to protect himself.

Too late.

With a howl of triumph, the vampire thrust the log forward—and shoved it through Billy's chest.

Chapter 21

DEAD ON THE SAND

Billy gasped and staggered back.

His legs collapsed, and he dropped to his knees on the sand.

He waited for the pain, for the crushing pain to sweep over his body. He waited for the darkness . . .

He glanced down at his chest, expecting to see the gaping wound. To his surprise, he saw no wound staining his shirt.

Instead he saw that the driftwood had crumbled. The log, soft and decayed, had fallen to pieces when it struck his chest. Tiny, burning chunks glowed on the sand in front of him.

Billy sucked in a deep breath of fresh ocean air. I'm alive, he thought. I'm alive—and I'm not giving this vampire another chance.

With a cry of rage, he rushed at Jon.

The vampire opened his fanged mouth in an angry hiss.

Billy leapt at him. Dug his fingers into the vampire's bony shoulders. Pushed him. Pushed him back.

Back.

The vampire hissed again and lowered his fangs to Billy's throat.

Driven by a rage he had never felt before, Billy pushed him. Back. Back.

And with a burst of strength, he heaved the startled vampire onto the purple, burning embers of the fire.

Jon landed hard on his back. The fire sizzled beneath him.

The vampire's eyes flared red. He shot his hands up to the sky as if reaching for something to pull himself up.

His mouth opened in a silent cry as the flames leapt around him.

And then, as Billy gaped in amazement, black smoke rose up from the sand. Billows of black smoke surrounded the thrashing vampire.

Billy took a step back, his heart pounding, his legs weak.

The smoke billowed into a thick curtain. It darkened the sky and the beach.

Behind the black curtain, Billy heard a fluttering sound. The fluttering became louder. Billy recognized the flap of wings.

Bat wings.

A red-eyed bat flapped up from behind the smoke. It rose over Billy, its tiny, round eyes glaring angrily. Dripping yellow saliva, the mouth opened in a shrill, menacing hiss.

And then the bat flapped away, swooping rapidly out over the sand, out to the ocean.

Billy stood watching it, swallowing hard, choking back his fear, his face drenched with sweat despite the coolness of the night.

Breathing hard, his chest heaving, he turned to Lynette. She hadn't moved, he saw to his horror. She lay lifelessly, sprawled on her back in the cold, wet sand.

"Hey!" A familiar voice made Billy jump.

He turned to see Nate and Irene running toward him across the sand. Nate, so big and powerful, came charging over the sand like an angry bull.

"What are you doing here? Where's Lynette?" he called to Billy.

Nate stopped a few feet from Billy. His mouth opened in a startled cry when he saw his sister on the sand.

"No—!" Nate cried, turning accusingly to Billy. "Oh no! What did you *do* to her?"

"Nothing!" Billy screamed. "I didn't—"

Nate dropped down beside Lynette on the sand. "No!" he cried. "No! Oh no! She's dead!"

Chapter 22

IS BILLY CRAZY?

Nate jumped to his feet, his features twisted in a rage. With a frightening roar, he grabbed Billy by the shoulders.

"No—stop!" Irene pleaded.

"What did you do to her?" Nate shrieked, spitting in Billy's face in his fury. "Are you sick? Are you *sick?"*

A low groan from the sand made everyone freeze.

Billy turned and saw Lynette's eyelids flutter. She turned her head and groaned again.

"She's alive!" Nate cried happily. He let go of Billy and dropped down beside her again. "Lynette? Are you okay? Did Billy hurt you?"

She gazed up, dazed, still unable to speak.

"I didn't do anything!" Billy insisted shrilly.

"It was that vampire. I tried to save her from that vampire!"

Nate glared up at him. "I'm warning you, Billy. Get away from here," he said through clenched teeth.

"I warned you that Jon was a vampire," Billy told Nate. "He dragged Lynette here. But I fought him off. I didn't hurt her, Nate. I saved her life. You've got to believe me!"

Billy heard Irene utter a "tsk-tsk" behind him.

"You're crazy, Billy," Nate cried, still on his knees beside his sister. "All this vampire talk is crazy. And sick. You left the mental hospital too soon. You're still sick. Now, get away from here. Go get help. Get yourself some help. Or I'll pound you. I really will."

"You've got to believe me!" Billy pleaded. "You've—"

Lynette opened her eyes wide. She sat up groggily, staring around. "Where am I?"

"Lynette will tell you the whole thing," Billy insisted desperately. "Lynette will tell you about Jon, about how he dragged her out here to the beach."

Nate leaned over his sister. "Is it true?"

"Tell him," Billy pleaded. "Tell him, Lynette. Tell him about the vampire."

Lynette blinked several times. She shook her

head hard as if trying to see clearly. "I . . . can't remember," she said finally in a tiny voice.

"Tell him what happened. Please!" Billy insisted.

"I was in Swanny's," Lynette said, thinking hard. "I was playing a Ninja Turtles game. And . . . that's all I remember."

"You don't remember Jon?" Billy demanded weakly. "Tell him about Jon, Lynette. About the tall boy dressed in black. He pulled you out here to the beach—remember?"

Lynette shook her head. "I remember seeing him in Swanny's. But I don't remember anything else." Tears welled in her eyes. "I don't remember coming out here."

Nate turned accusingly to Billy.

"She doesn't remember because Jon clouded her mind," Billy told him. "He clouded her mind. That's why she was lying unconscious on the beach. The vampire—"

"I'm going to cloud *your* mind!" Nate cried, jumping to his feet.

"It was the vampire!" Billy screamed. "You've got to believe—"

He didn't finish his frantic cry—because Nate's fist came crashing into his jaw.

Chapter 23

A PAIN IN THE NECK

Billy walked alone through town the next evening.

Fog floated low and thick over the street, hiding Sandy Hollow behind a misty white curtain. It pressed in on Billy, closing him inside his own private cloud.

He rubbed his sore jaw. His thoughts were bitter.

No one believes me, he told himself. Everyone thinks I'm crazy. I'm totally alone.

Something cool and damp grabbed his foot.

It oozed around the straps of his thongs.

Billy glanced down in surprise. Wet sand. He had reached the beach without realizing it.

Pulling off his thongs, he went barefoot, enjoying the feel of the sand as it squished up between his toes. The waves crashed against the stone jetty somewhere off to his left.

Flapping.

From behind him.

Billy spun around. This time he would be ready for the bats. But he saw only one. It swooped past him and continued on its way, a black speck in the fog.

Lost in his own thoughts, Billy drifted along the beach.

Now he heard another sound.

Behind him.

Someone following him!

He spun around.

No one there.

I'm letting myself get spooked, he concluded. There's no one here but me.

Billy took another step. Stopped.

A shape stood in front of him.

Shimmering in the fog.

"Who's there?" he asked.

"Just me," Kylie replied, stepping into focus.

"I—I didn't see you come up. What are you doing out here?" he asked.

"I didn't feel like being home alone. Mind if I walk with you?"

"No. Of course not."

They strolled along the beach, surrounded on all sides by a misty white wall of fog.

Kylie grabbed his arm. "Listen. Hear that?"

"A foghorn."

"I love that sound, don't you?"

"It's sort of mysterious," Billy replied.

Kylie stepped in front of him. She reached out and slipped her arms around his neck. "I love the fog," she whispered. "No one can see us."

Billy gazed into her eyes, thinking how beautiful Kylie was. Beautiful Kylie. Her perfect face framed by all that red hair. Her eyes seeming to shimmer even in the fog.

She kissed him. Long and slow.

I have no time for this, Billy thought. *I have to find April. I have to save Jay.*

Chapter 24

KISSES FOR JAY

"Ouch!" Billy pulled away. "What was that?" He rubbed his neck.

"Probably a mosquito," Kylie said. "They always come out when it's so wet."

"Sorry I jumped like that," Billy told her.

"I hate mosquitoes," she said. "Such miserable little bloodsuckers."

Billy rubbed the spot. "I have to get home," he told Kylie.

"You're always running off," she complained.

"I'm sorry. But I really have to call Jay. I'm kind of worried about him."

She leaned against him. "Maybe we can get together tomorrow night?"

"Sure," Billy replied. "Or the night after.

Where are you headed? I'll walk part of the way with you."

"Thanks, but I think I'm going to walk on the beach for a while."

Billy started toward his house. Glancing behind him, he saw that Kylie had already disappeared in the fog. A moment later a loud sound startled him.

A hissing screech.

Full of rage.

A cat?

A bat flapped over his head. Billy glanced up, but the creature was invisible in the fog.

Billy tried to phone Jay as soon as he got home. No answer.

He climbed into bed, thinking about Kylie—about her hot, hot kisses.

Am I crazy? he wondered. *Most guys would jump at the chance to go out with such a beautiful girl.*

But I can't get too close, he decided. *I can't forget why I came back to Sandy Hollow.*

That vampire came too close to hurting Lynette.

And April is too close to Jay. That's more important than all Kylie's kisses.

I can't let Jay become a vampire.

* * *

Jay sat on the beach, listening to the waves tumble and roar as they slid over the jetty and rolled onto the sand. The sound was distant, like a dream.

A girl slipped her arms around his neck.

Was she really there?

Or was she imaginary, nothing but wisps of fog?

She kissed his face. Then his lips.

"April," he whispered. "April."

The fog seemed to be lifting. Only patches now. Moonlight twinkled on the surface of the waves. Everything shimmered. Everything.

Jay tried to focus on the girl. The waves reflected the moonlight, making dancing lights in her hair. She seemed fuzzy, unreal.

Why was everything such a blur?

She kissed him. Again and again.

A gentle breeze stirred the night air, clearing away the last wisps of fog. But that one spot, right where he sat with the girl, seemed covered in mist.

Her kisses continued, as if they would go on forever. Yes, he thought. Forever. Forever.

He whispered her name again. "April."

Her lips left his, sliding down to his neck.

Jay felt twin stabs of pain in his throat.

But they seemed far, far away.

Part of a dream.

Not real.

"April," he murmured. "April, what are you doing to me?"

Chapter 25

BUG BITES

Billy drifted along Main Street, scanning the faces of the people coming in and out of brightly lighted shops, hoping to spot Jay.

He had been phoning Jay's condo endlessly. But no one answered. He had to assume the worst—that Jay was with April.

He knew Jay was under April's spell.

April had clouded Jay's mind.

Her hold on him would be hard to break.

I have to keep trying, Billy thought grimly. I can't give up. I can never give up.

A blond girl and a muscular boy with sandy hair stepped out of an antique store.

"Nate!" he called, hurrying toward them. "Irene!"

Two strangers turned to him with puzzled expressions on their faces.

Billy mumbled an apology, and the couple hurried away.

Where is everyone? Billy wondered. Why can't I find my friends?

He checked the beach. At least it wasn't foggy tonight. The moonlight made it easy to see everyone there. But he spotted only a few couples. No one he recognized.

He had thought a lot about how to destroy April. He knew he had to get her into the sun. Or drive a stake through her heart while she slept. But how could he do it alone?

If Jay would help him, he knew he stood a chance. Then there would be a way.

Billy decided to check Jay's condo. He made his way to the row of condos, found Jay's place, and rang the bell several times.

Nobody home.

He stood on Jay's doorstep, trying to figure out where everyone could have gone. He pushed the doorbell button again even though he knew he was wasting his time. He heard its muffled ringing from inside the empty condo.

Billy almost jumped when the door opened.

Jay gazed at him through half-shut eyes. He appeared weak and pale, as if he might fall down at any moment.

"Man, you look really awful!" Billy exclaimed.

"I *feel* awful."

Billy stepped inside. No one else there. "Where are your parents?" he asked.

"They're having dinner with some people they met on the beach. I couldn't go. I think I'd hurl if I tried to eat anything."

They sat down on the couch.

"Were you out partying last night?" Billy asked.

"Last night?" Jay frowned. "I don't think I was out too late. I can't remember. I went walking on the beach with April, and everything else is sort of . . . foggy."

Billy studied his friend. So pale. So fragile-looking.

Nothing on Jay's neck, but Billy knew the mark of the vampire was there, below the collar, out of sight.

"You can't remember because a vampire clouded your mind," Billy declared.

Jay shook his head. "Not that vampire junk again," he groaned.

"I'll show you!" Billy cried. "I'll make you believe me!"

He yanked Jay's collar down so hard the top button of his polo shirt popped off and sailed across the room.

"Hey!" Jay protested. "What are you doing?"

"There!" Billy announced. "I knew it!"

Two marks in the soft flesh of Jay's neck.

Red. Swollen.

Puncture holes.

"Look at your neck!" Billy cried. "Look at the bite marks!" He dragged Jay to a mirror.

"What about my neck?"

"Look at it! Don't you see it?"

"See *what,* man? I don't know what you're talking about."

"The bite marks."

Jay sighed. "You want me to believe that those bug bites are vampire bites?"

"Those are puncture marks."

"Those are bug bites!" Jay cried impatiently. "All this vampire talk is crazy, Billy. It's bad enough being sick during summer vacation. I don't need you cracking up again. I can't deal with this!"

"I'm trying to save you before it's too late. Before you become one of them."

"I'm not too worried, Billy. I've had lots of bug bites, and I haven't turned into a bug yet."

"April has messed up your mind so you don't see things clearly. They can do that, Jay. So when you look in the mirror you see bug bites. That's what she *wants* you to see."

Jay glared at him. "April? You think April is a vampire? You're crazy! You leave April out of this. She's the first girl who ever liked me. If you ruin it for me—"

"Listen to me," Billy interrupted. "I know why you've felt so bad lately. When April drinks your blood, she leaves behind some of her poison. It makes you sick. And eventually it will turn you into one of *them*—a vampire!"

Jay let out a hoarse cry. "Right. And if I go out during a full moon, I'll become a werewolf."

"I'm serious, Jay! You're in a lot of danger. If April drinks your blood one more time . . . that might be all it takes!"

"Leave me alone, man," Jay snapped. "Take a hike. Really. You're totally disturbed."

"I'm trying to help you!" Billy yelled. Anger surged through him. How can I make Jay listen? How can I make him see what's happening to him?

"Get out of here, Billy!" Jay repeated.

Billy leapt to his feet. "I tried," Billy said with a sigh. "I tried."

He whirled around and stormed out the door. I have to prove it, Billy decided. I have to find some way to prove I'm right.

How do you *prove* to someone that his girlfriend is a vampire?

"Hi, Billy," whispered a husky voice.

Billy raised his eyes to Kylie. She grinned at him.

"Where did you come from?" he asked in surprise.

"I was right here all the time," she answered. "There's a barbecue on the beach. Want to go?"

"Sure," he answered.

"Good," Kylie replied. She slipped her arm through his and licked her lips. "I'm starving."

Chapter 26

BILLY'S BIG NIGHT

April pushed the sand around with her bare toes. The sun had set half an hour ago, but the sand still felt warm against her foot. She heard voices. Glanced up. A boy and girl strolled along the beach, chatting.

Kylie and Irene had pulled her aside at the barbecue last night. The three of them had agreed to meet tonight on the beach as soon as it turned dark. To compare notes on how their bet was going.

Kylie and Irene were half an hour late. April wondered if they had forgotten. After all, they had been sort of distracted at the barbecue last night.

April grinned, thinking about it. She had enjoyed watching Kylie and Billy. Kylie did everything she could to get his attention. But Billy seemed distracted, upset about something. Kylie had been really angry, and it showed.

I'm surprised she didn't grab him and bite his neck right there, April thought.

Bats flapped overhead. April gazed up, thinking it might be Kylie and Irene. But they were just bats, flying from the island for a night of feasting on the mainland bugs.

It was a clear night. The moon was no longer full, but it still shone brightly. April could see the beach clearly.

She spotted two figures approaching across a large dune. Kylie and Irene.

"You're late," she informed them when they reached her.

"So what?" Kylie asked. "You're immortal. What's a little time to you?"

"We're going to be late for play practice if we don't hurry," April said.

"Kylie doesn't care," Irene stated. "I told her we were late, but she had to try on three different pairs of shorts and half a dozen tops."

Kylie yawned.

"It's too bad we can't see our reflections in the mirror," Irene went on. "Poor Kylie really misses admiring herself."

"At least I've got something to admire," Kylie shot back.

"Will you give me a break," April begged. "I don't want to waste the whole night while the two of you snap at each other. I'm hungry."

"She's right," Irene agreed. "We're supposed to be comparing notes."

"Okay," Kylie replied. "How are you two doing?"

April grinned. "I'm going to get Jay alone after play practice tonight."

Irene shook her head disgustedly. "I haven't gotten Nate alone long enough to get a sip. His bratty little sister is always tagging along! I'm so happy his parents took her home. They said she was having nightmares about vampires!"

April shook her head.

"You're both going to lose," Kylie declared. "Billy doesn't suspect a thing. I've been taking it slow." She smiled, showing the tips of her needle-sharp fangs. "But tonight is his big night."

PART FOUR

VAMPIRE TRAP

Chapter 27

APRIL IS CAUGHT

"Don't even talk to me," Jay told Billy as soon as he entered the theater for play practice. "I don't want to hear any more talk about vampires—unless you're talking about the play."

"Jay"—Billy began. But his friend strode away across the stage. Billy watched him, knowing he couldn't give up, no matter how angry Jay got. I have to keep trying, Billy thought.

Rehearsal was late getting started. Some of the kids hadn't shown up yet—including Kylie, Irene, and April. Ms. Aaronson paced back and forth along the front of the stage, glancing at her watch.

Billy shifted his attention back to Jay. He looks even worse, Billy saw. Jay's eyes were glazed and watery. He was so pale he was totally white, as if he'd never been in the sun in his entire life.

Like a vampire.

How many more sips before Jay became one of them?

After rehearsal, Ms. Aaronson asked Nate and Irene to stay for a few moments so they could work on their scenes.

Billy spotted Jay and April leaving together through the main exit. He started to go after them, but someone blocked his path.

"It's nice out," Kylie told him. "Want to take a walk?"

"Yeah," Billy replied. "Let's catch up with April and Jay."

They stepped out of the theater, and Billy looked around for Jay and April. He spotted a boy and girl making out by the corner of the building. Kids were strolling toward town on the narrow road. Others headed directly for the beach.

No sign of Jay.

Had April lured him behind the theater? Into the woods?

Was she drinking his blood at that very moment?

"Come on," Kylie urged. "Let's go into town."

Billy scanned the sidewalks as he followed her,

searching for Jay and April. He saw kids holding hands. Eating hot dogs. Checking out the window of the Beach Emporium.

"Do you want to rehearse our scene?" Kylie asked.

"I only say a few words," Billy muttered. "They're not hard to remember."

"But I've got a lot of dialogue to memorize," Kylie reminded him. "I could use the help."

"Okay," Billy agreed. "But I don't have my script. I left it at the theater."

"Run back and get it," Kylie said. "I'll meet you on the beach by the wooden steps."

Billy trotted back to the theater. He expected to find Nate and Irene still going over their scenes with Ms. Aaronson. But the theater was dark.

Bet Ms. Aaronson locked it up, Billy thought. He tried the door.

It opened easily. Billy stepped inside the lobby, letting the door slam behind him. The theater was black. He felt his way along the wall.

Billy tried to remember where the light switch was. He pictured the lobby in his mind. The ticket booth. A Coke machine. The doors leading to the seats. Where was the light switch?

A noise. Off to his left. A click.

"Who's there?" he called.

No one answered.

Billy's heart began to hammer in his chest.

Why is the theater open but all the lights off? he wondered.

He slammed against something big and hard. It clanked and rattled.

The Coke machine.

Billy let out his breath. He went back to searching for the light switch.

Another sound. A soft patter. It seemed to echo off the walls and surround him.

"Hello?" he called, surprised at how shaky his voice sounded.

Get a hold of yourself, he thought. It's probably just mice.

He moved along the wall, feeling for a light switch. Finally his fingers found the edge of a switch plate. Then the switch itself. He flipped it up.

The overhead lights came on.

Billy blinked rapidly, trying to adjust to the sudden brightness. He took in his surroundings. He stood in the lobby. Alone. If there had been mice, they had scurried for cover the moment the lights came on.

The rest rooms, Billy thought.

Was someone hiding in the rest rooms?

He pushed open the door of the men's room and stepped inside. Empty. He tried the women's room. No one there either.

Okay, he told himself, quit this messing around and get your script. Kylie is going to wonder what happened to you.

He stepped through the double doors into the auditorium. Rows of empty seats stretched out in front of him. All facing the empty stage.

His footsteps echoed in the deserted theater as he walked slowly toward the stage.

He had left his script in the wings, on a wooden stool.

He started up the steps to the stage. A large bundle of cloth lay on the floor toward the rear of the stage. Billy glanced at the material. Gray streaks on it. Familiar gray streaks.

It was a backdrop painting of a grimy basement where the vampires kept their coffins.

It had taken some of the kids hours to paint it. Who would have rolled it up like that and tossed it to side of the stage?

Billy hurried over to the backdrop. I should spread it out, he decided. It will get wrinkled if it is left all bunched up like that.

He grabbed the edge of the backdrop and pulled hard.

To his surprise, the cloth had not been rolled up. Merely placed on top of something.

On top of what? Billy wondered.

He peered down—and saw the body.

A woman's body.

Billy felt his stomach tighten into a hard knot.

"No!" he gasped.

Ms. Aaronson. Sprawled on her back. Her face as gray as the backdrop that had covered her.

Billy climbed shakily to his feet. He leaned over her—and saw the two bite marks on her neck.

Not another one, Billy thought. Another vampire murder.

A movement caught Billy's eye.

Was the vampire still here?

His heart pounding, he spun around.

And saw a figure hiding in the shadows.

April.

Chapter 28

APRIL AND BILLY

She stood in the deep shadows, near the back of the stage. Her eyes wide. Her mouth open.

Fangs! Billy thought. Are her fangs still down?

April's hands flew up to cover her mouth. She made a gagging sound and turned away from the pale body on the stage.

Should I tell her? Billy thought. Should I tell her she doesn't have to pretend in front of me?

Should I tell her I know she is a vampire?

No. She knows that I know.

Billy strode across the stage to where April stood. He grasped her arm and spun her around.

April gave a little shriek when her gaze fell on the body. She took a stumbling step backward.

"What are you doing here?" Billy asked her. "I thought you were with Jay."

"I was," April said. Her breathing came in sharp gasps. "But he was too tired. He had to go home. I came back to the theater because I wanted to ask Ms. Aaronson something. But I . . ." Her voice trailed off.

She stood there, trembling, pretending to be bewildered and scared.

She killed Ms. Aaronson, Billy knew. Just as she killed the others.

"I just got here," April insisted. "Only a minute ago. I came in and found Ms. Aaronson. Then I heard a noise. And I hid—because I thought it was the killer. I was so terrified. But it turned out to be you."

"I'm going to call the police," Billy told her.

She nodded.

Billy ran to the phone in the lobby and dialed 911. The dispatcher promised to have an officer there in a few minutes. The police will be *thrilled* to see me again, Billy thought bitterly.

He slammed the phone down. Turned—and found April standing a few feet behind him. His stomach tightened.

It suddenly dawned on him.

She's a vampire. And I'm alone with her.

Billy tried to move back.

Banged into the wall.

April's eyes locked onto his. She took a step forward.

Another.

"Billy," she whispered. "Billy . . ."

Chapter 29

BILLY SETS A TRAP

April threw herself into his arms. "Would you hold me? I can't stop shaking. Just hold me?"

For a moment, Billy stood still. *Is this a trick?* he wondered. *Does she plan to attack me, too?* Then his arms automatically closed around her.

She really is trembling, he saw.

And cold . . . her skin is so cold.

Cold as death. The phrase repeated in Billy's mind. *Cold as death.*

Vampires are already dead.

April pulled back and gazed at Billy. He imagined her fangs sliding down. Her lips pulling back from her teeth.

Her fangs piercing his skin.

A siren shrieked outside the theater. Billy gave a sigh of relief. The police had arrived.

Was that disappointment on April's face?

"The police are talking about closing the beach and sending everybody home," Billy announced. He, Jay, and Nate were skipping stones over the water.

It had been three days since Ms. Aaronson's murder. No killer had been found. No connection between the deaths. No official word on how they had all died.

But the police know, Billy thought. They would never close the beach unless they knew about the vampires.

He had promised Jay that he wouldn't mention vampires anymore. Billy and Nate had made an uneasy truce. But Billy knew that Nate wouldn't put up with any vampire talk, either.

At least Jay hasn't gotten any weaker, Billy thought. He still looks terrible. But April must be leaving him alone.

For now.

Frustrated, Billy picked up a round, flat stone and skipped it off the top of a breaker as it rolled into shore.

Nate tried to imitate him. But Nate's stone went *plop* and vanished into the ocean. "How come yours skip and mine sink?" he asked.

"Skill," Billy replied.

Jay chuckled. But Billy knew it was forced laughter. Nothing seemed funny lately. Not after so many people had died.

"Will they really close the beach?" Jay asked.

"Wow," Nate said, shaking his head. "You mean we'd all have to go home?"

"That's right," Billy replied.

"But I have the condo to myself now that my parents took Lynette home," Nate complained. "If they send us home, I'd have to give it up. And I'll have to say goodbye to Irene."

It's better than seeing her murdered by vampires, Billy thought.

"Speaking of Irene," Nate said, glancing at his watch, "I'm supposed to meet her at the Beach Emporium. Catch you guys later."

Billy watched Nate trot down the beach. Then he turned to Jay.

"Did April tell you that Ms. Aaronson had bite marks on her neck?" he asked.

Jay kept walking. He didn't answer.

"I saw them," Billy insisted. "Did April say anything about it?"

"No," Jay answered. "Now drop it!"

Billy grabbed Jay's arm and pulled him to a stop. "Let me prove to you that April is a vampire—before she makes you one, too. I know a way to prove it."

"Oh, please," Jay moaned. "Give me a break."

"You know you're sick," Billy pressed on.

"I've got the flu or something."

"How about your neck?" Billy demanded. "Have those 'bug bites' gotten any better? Or are they worse?"

Jay groaned.

"If I can prove it, you have to believe me," Billy insisted. "And if I don't prove it, I'll shut up. I'll never say another word about vampires. And I'll leave April alone."

"Fine!" Jay yelled. "I give up! You won't drop this until I let you try, will you? Okay, go ahead. But don't blame me if you end up looking like a total jerk."

Great! Billy thought. Finally.

"What are you going to do?" Jay asked.

"First, you have to promise not to be alone with April until this is over," Billy told him.

"You're kidding, right?"

"Look, Jay, she's already bitten you once or twice. Three times and you're a vampire."

"I'm not going to quit seeing April."

"You don't have to. You just have to make sure someone else is there whenever you're with April."

"That's just what I need—a chaperone."

"Jay—"

"Okay, okay. I'll do it."

"Promise?"

"Yes, I promise. Tell me what you're planning to do."

"It's easy," Billy explained. "What kills vampires?"

"I'm not driving a stake through April's heart."

"We don't have to do that. What else kills them?"

"I don't know."

"Sunlight."

"Sunlight," Jay repeated.

Billy leaned forward to explain exactly what he had in mind. When he was almost finished, he heard a sound behind him.

He turned quickly. And saw April standing behind him. Her eyes burned into Billy's.

How long has she been standing there? Billy asked himself.

How much did she hear?

Chapter 30

GOODBYE TO A VAMPIRE

"Hey—what's up?" April said cheerfully. "I thought I might find you guys here."

Billy studied her face, trying to tell if she had overheard his plan.

She stepped close to Jay. "You guys just hanging out? Want to take a walk or something?"

Jay glanced at Billy. "I can't," he told April. "I'm still feeling really wrecked."

"I've got to get home, too," Billy told her.

"Okay," April replied. "Maybe I'll see you guys tomorrow sometime." She turned and started toward Main Street. "Oh," she cried, turning around. "I almost forgot. There's going to be a huge clambake on the beach tomorrow. Want to go?"

"Sounds excellent," Jay answered.

"See you then," April replied.

"It's okay." Billy sighed as soon as April had disappeared from view. "She didn't overhear our plan."

"She *better* not have," Jay growled. "If you mess things up between April and me, I'll never forgive you. Really."

"Hey man, where've you been?" Jay asked as Billy joined him the next night on the beach. "The clams are all gone."

Billy shrugged. "I got hung up. I'll pick up a burger somewhere."

"Hey, Billy," April called. She and Jay sat on the sand with some other kids.

It was well after midnight, and the beach party had spread out all over the beach. Billy was relieved that Jay seemed to be keeping his promise not to be alone with April.

He surveyed the scene. Kids talking and tipping back cans of soda. A pyramid constructed from the empties—six feet tall and growing. A group of guys and girls trying to play volleyball with a glow-in-the-dark ball. The steamy aroma of charcoal smoke and clams lingered in the air.

Tonight is the night, Billy thought.

Tonight is your *last* night, April.

He had to trick April into going somewhere

with Jay—but not just anywhere. It had to be a place without windows.

And then he had to keep April there until dawn. Until the sun came up.

Lightning flashed out over the ocean. Followed by a distant rumble of thunder. Dark, billowing clouds filled the night sky.

Rain, Billy thought. If it rains, my plan will work. If it rains, I can get April to go inside. And stay there until the sun comes up.

Billy saw that Kylie had joined them. She stood between Nate and Jay, listening to their conversation.

Rain, Billy thought. Please rain.

Kylie slipped beside Billy. "Let's go for a walk along the beach," she whispered in his ear.

"No. Sit down. I don't feel like walking right now," Billy told her.

I've got to stay close to Jay, he thought. So I can make sure April doesn't manage to get him alone. And I've got to be ready.

Kylie's eyes locked onto his, and Billy felt the urge to go with her. But he resisted. "I just want to hang out with everyone," he said.

Kylie lowered her eyes. Billy realized she was pouting.

Another rumble in the distance. More thunder.

Black clouds rolled low over the sky.

Please rain, Billy urged again.

But the thunder and lightning remained in the distance.

By three in the morning, the clambake had become a wild party.

"I think everyone is trying to forget about the murders," Kylie commented. Billy nodded.

"Billy, can we please go for a walk?" she asked again. "I don't know why you want to sit in one place all night."

Billy sighed. But his answer was lost in a sudden clap of thunder. He glanced up to see a flash of lightning rip through the sky directly overhead, followed by another rumble of thunder.

The downpour came an instant later.

Kids scurried for cover, shrieking and laughing. "Billy!" Kylie cried. "This way!" She sprinted toward Main Street with a group of kids.

Perfect!

Billy turned to Jay. "Let's do it," he said.

Jay nodded grimly. "April, come on," he shouted over the noise of the rain. "The theater is the closest place."

The two of them dashed for the theater. Billy followed. Rain pelted him, the wind-driven drops stinging his eyes. Billy glanced over his shoulder. Good. No one behind them.

He sped past Jay and yanked open the theater door.

April and Jay rushed inside as lightning sizzled overhead and a thunderclap shook the building.

They stood in the lobby, breathing hard. "What a wild storm!" April exclaimed. "I'm drenched."

"Me too!" Jay cried, stamping his feet. He looks totally wiped out, Billy saw. That run must have been too much for him.

"Let's go down to the basement," Billy suggested. "It's warmer down there."

The sign on the door to the basement read THEATER PERSONNEL ONLY, but it was never locked. Billy flipped on the light, and they started down a set of wooden steps.

Billy closed the door behind him. The basement had two exits. The one they had entered through. And the one that led directly outside.

No windows.

The perfect place, Billy thought.

It was crammed with props that had been used in plays over the years. Costumes covered in clear plastic hung on a rack along one wall. Hat boxes lined the shelf above it. One was marked ENGLISH TOP HAT. Another read GIRLS' BONNETS.

Billy sat down on a wooden box. April and Jay found a couple of stools. Now I stall for time, Billy thought. We've got to keep April here until sunrise.

They were all soaked. April fussed with her soggy hair. Billy saw that April was not wearing a watch. Everything was working out perfectly.

An icy look from Jay. Hang in there, Billy thought. I know you don't like tricking April. But you'll see that I'm right—the minute the sunlight hits her.

They talked for a while. But Jay seemed too tired to keep up much of a conversation.

"What time is it?" April finally asked.

"Three-fifteen," Billy lied, glancing at his watch. It was really much later—almost daybreak. Another few minutes, he thought. And the vampire will be history.

"I'd better go soon," she told Jay. "I'll really be in trouble if I don't get home before dawn."

You sure will, Billy thought. "You can't go out in this storm," he protested.

"We can't even tell if it's still raining," she complained. "There aren't any windows. Let's go upstairs."

"The storm couldn't be over this soon," Billy insisted. "Not the way it was coming down."

"I'll go upstairs and check," April declared.

"Let's send Jay instead," Billy suggested. "He'll fall asleep if he doesn't move."

April chuckled. "Yeah, go see if it's still raining," she told Jay. "And get me a Coke while you're there?"

Jay hesitated. Come on, Billy thought. Don't quit on me now.

Jay stood up slowly. He trudged up the stairs. He looked half dead.

He returned five minutes later with three cans of Coke. "It's still coming down," he announced, handing the drinks around. He nodded to Billy.

Billy knew what that meant. The rain had actually stopped. The sun had come up.

Time for April's test. A test Billy knew she would flunk.

"It's time," he announced.

He grabbed April. Coke sloshed out of her can and onto her T-shirt.

"What are you doing?" she demanded sharply. "Let go of me!" She dropped the can. Liquid squirted out, spattering his shoes.

Jay stood still, staring at April.

"Go on, Jay!" Billy shouted. "Open the door!"

"Billy!" April screamed. "Let me go!"

Jay strode to the door leading outside, turned the knob—and glanced back at April.

"Jay!" she cried. "Help me!"

Billy dragged her to the door. "Open it!" he instructed Jay.

April fought fiercely, kicking, scratching. Trying desperately to wriggle out of his grasp. "What are you *doing?* Let me go!"

Jay yanked open the door, revealing concrete steps leading up to ground level. Bright sunlight reflected off the steps.

April gasped. "You said it was still raining!" she cried. "What's going on here? What are you *doing?"*

She struggled fiercely to get away from Billy. He tightened his grip on her arms.

And shoved her through the open door.

Into the sun.

April screamed. Sunlight streamed over her.

And Billy watched her head burst into flame.

Chapter 31

APRIL IS DEAD

Billy gasped and shut his eyes. He could see the white light through his eyelids.

When he opened his eyes again, he cried out in shock.

April stood bathed in bright sunlight, staring back at him angrily.

"Huh?" Billy's mouth dropped open. April hadn't exploded, hadn't burst into flame.

Had he imagined it? Had he *wanted* it so much that he hallucinated it?

Her blond hair glowed in the bright morning sunlight. She glared at Billy, shielding her eyes with one hand. "Satisfied?" she demanded in a whisper. "Satisfied?"

Jay gave Billy a hard shove that sent him into the concrete wall. "You jerk," Jay snapped. "You stupid jerk. You almost had me believing you."

Billy opened his mouth to reply—but couldn't find the words.

April shook her head. She stepped past them both, back into the basement. "I'm not a vampire," she said flatly. "You guys satisfied?"

Jay scowled at Billy. "You really are messed up, man. You really need help." He shoved Billy again.

"Guys, give me a break," April murmured. "You're going to ruin everything."

She dropped wearily onto a tall stool. Billy and Jay sat down across from her. "You're going to ruin everything I've worked so hard on," April said with a sigh.

"I—I don't understand," Billy stammered. "I thought I did. But I don't understand anything."

"You're sick," Jay insisted, still scowling at him. "I feel like such a jerk for listening to you. I'm really sorry, April. I knew you weren't a vampire. There's no such thing as vampires. But Billy kept after me. He wouldn't give it a rest. He—"

"But there *are* vampires here!" April interrupted heatedly. "That's why I'm here. That's why I've pretended to *be* a vampire."

"April—" Billy started.

"My name isn't April," she revealed. "It's Diana. Diana Devlin. April Blair was my cousin."

"Your cousin?" Billy cried.

"My cousin and my best friend," Diana revealed sadly. Her voice caught on the words.

"What happened to April?" Billy asked softly.

"She came here last summer," Diana replied, staring at the floor. "The vampires got her. They turned her into one of them. April confided in me. She knew she could trust me. She . . ." Diana's voice broke.

She cleared her throat and started again, still keeping her eyes lowered. "When she came back to Shadyside after the summer, April was a vampire. She hated it. She hated what she had become—a creature, not a person. A creature who feeds on other people.

"She told me all about it. At first, I didn't believe it. But she made me believe. And then, I felt so helpless. There was nothing I could do for her. No way I could help her.

"Finally, April solved her problem for herself. The only way she could." A tear slid down Diana's cheek. "One morning she stepped out into the sunlight. She killed herself."

"Wow. Oh wow," Jay murmured sadly, shaking his head.

Silence for a while.

Billy broke the silence. "Why are you here?" he asked Diana. "Why did you take April's name? Why did you come to Sandy Hollow this summer?"

"I came back to kill the vampires who murdered my cousin," Diana replied through gritted teeth. She wiped another tear off her cheek. "I want to pay them back for what they did to April. I want to kill them all!

"They believe I'm April," she continued. "I look a lot like my cousin. They believe I'm April. And they believe I'm a vampire."

She sighed. "I've had a couple of close calls. That boy Rick—he almost ruined everything."

Billy remembered Rick. He had found Rick's body—his drained body—in the sand that same night.

"But Rick recognized you as April!" Billy said.

Diana shook her head. "No. He recognized me as *Diana.* He almost ruined everything. That's why I dragged him away as fast as I could. Before he could call me by my real name."

"And then—you *killed* him?" Billy gasped. "To keep your secret?"

Diana narrowed her eyes at him. "Of course not. I'm not a murderer. I didn't kill Rick. I think Kylie did."

Billy jumped to his feet. His heart thudded in

his chest. His whole body shook. "Kylie?" he cried shrilly.

Diana nodded solemnly. "Kylie and Irene are vampires," she revealed. Her eyes burned into Billy's. "You didn't guess that? You really didn't?"

Billy felt too shocked to reply. He shook his head, murmuring the two names. "Kylie? Irene?"

"I think Kylie killed that girl Mae-Linn. And she killed Rick."

"But—why?" Billy demanded.

"For the nectar. Kylie wasn't getting anywhere with you, Billy. And she was so thirsty."

"I can't believe this," Jay chimed in, shaking his head. "I can't believe we're sitting here talking about people we know being vampires. I must be dreaming this. I have to be dreaming!"

"I wish," Diana murmured sadly. "But Kylie and Irene really are vampires. And I have fooled them into believing I'm one of them. I've fooled them so that I could get close enough to kill them both."

"Whoa. Wait a minute." Billy stepped forward to confront her. "There's only one problem with your story, Diana or April, or whoever you are."

Diana jumped to her feet. "Well?"

Billy pulled down Jay's shirt collar. "See these puncture holes? These aren't *pretend* holes, Diana. You've been hanging out with Jay, going out with him practically every night. And look at him. Look at this wound on his neck."

Billy's features hardened into anger. "How do you explain *that,* Diana? How do you explain what you've done to Jay?"

"I didn't do that," Diana insisted heatedly. "I don't have fangs. I don't drink blood. I think Kylie or Irene did it to Jay."

"But I haven't been with them!" Jay protested.

"I think one of them has been following you and me, Jay," Diana explained. "Probably Kylie. I think Kylie has been doing this to you—late at night after I leave."

"But I would know!" Jay cried. "I would see Kylie. I would recognize her!"

Diana shook her head. "No, you wouldn't. She clouded your mind. She probably made you think that she was *me.* I—I think Kylie killed Ms. Aaronson too. Just for the nectar. The vampire's thirst is so powerful. I've seen Kylie and Irene do such *disgusting* things—just to satisfy their thirst."

Billy shook his head. "Kylie. Kylie." He murmured her name again. "I came back to Sandy Hollow to kill vampires, too. But I never suspected her. I was so stupid . . ."

He thought about his walks alone with Kylie on the beach. He thought about her kisses.

And he shuddered.

"Let's go get them," he said to Diana. "We'll do it tomorrow. Let's find them while they're asleep in their coffins and kill them both."

"It won't be easy." Diana sighed.

She had no idea how right she was.

Chapter 32

RETURN TO VAMPIRE ISLAND

Raindrops pattered softly on the dock as Billy untied the line, then jumped into the rowboat with Diana. The boat rocked gently from side to side.

He and Diana wore raincoats with plastic hoods. Billy adjusted his hood as he settled into the boat.

I'm finally doing it, he thought. *I'm finally going to get my revenge on the vampires.*

It was only noon, but the dark clouds hovering low in the sky made it nearly as dark as night. Billy slipped the oars into the oarlocks and began rowing.

Diana sat in the stern, facing him. Her jaw was set, her expression determined, her eyes hard.

Billy was sure that nothing would stop her from killing Irene and Kylie if she got the chance.

He wished Jay had come along. He knew they needed all the help they could get. But after staying up all night the day before, poor, weakened Jay had to get some sleep.

Billy studied the two nylon backpacks that lay on the floor between them. Each one contained the same items. Wooden stakes. And a hammer. The tools for destroying vampires.

He had bought the stakes at a local carpenter shop. Made of the hardest oak, they were long and slender, tapered to an incredibly sharp point.

"I would feel better with bright sunlight," Diana declared.

"It's supposed to rain like this all week," Billy replied, dipping the oars into the water and leaning back as he pulled on the handles. "And I'm off from work today. This is the only day we can do it."

Diana nodded. "But it's such a dark day . . ."

"Most vampires can't stand *any* daylight," Billy assured her. "The sun doesn't have to be shining. That's what the books I read all say."

The rain continued to fall in a steady drizzle. The raindrops pattered on Billy's rain slicker. The ocean seemed as calm as a lake. The boat rocked gently as it glided toward the island.

"Are you scared?" Billy asked.

"Yes," Diana replied. "But I can do it. I've already killed one vampire. I know can do it again."

"You mean here?" Billy cried. "This summer?"

"Yes. His name was Eric. I killed him with a wooden stake."

Billy stared at her in astonishment. She looked so fragile and sweet. And she had already killed more vampires than he had. She didn't say anything more about it, so he didn't ask.

Glancing over his shoulder, Billy saw the island looming above them. This was the first time he had seen it in the daylight. It seemed dark and menacing even now.

"It looks evil," Diana observed.

"It *is* evil," Billy replied.

Before long he could make out the tall trees that lined the shore.

An icy drop of perspiration slid down his forehead. He shivered.

Billy rowed toward the spot where he thought the old dock stood. He scanned the shore.

Where's the dock? he wondered. Why can't I see it?

The boat drifted closer to shore.

"It's gone," he muttered.

"What is?" Diana asked. "What's gone?"

"The dock. Look."

A few sawed-off pilings poked out of the water, marking the spot where the dock had stood. He couldn't find a place to tie up the boat.

"Vampires must have destroyed the dock," Billy decided. "They wanted to make it harder for anyone to sneak up on them while they sleep."

Diana's eyes narrowed in fear. "Do you think the vampires suspect something? Do you think they might suspect someone is coming here to get them?"

It wasn't a question Billy wanted to think about.

He rowed along the shoreline, looking for a spot to beach the boat. There seemed to be nothing but big rocks and sheer drop-offs.

"Can we swim ashore?" Diana asked.

"No anchor. The boat would drift away. We'd have no way to get back."

Billy pulled on the oars, heading for the ocean side of the island. The waves grew bigger, the rowboat riding high on the swells, then dropping into the troughs. Ocean water burst over the bow, splashing into Billy's face.

"This little boat wasn't made for going into the ocean," Diana said tensely. She held onto her seat with both hands.

He spotted a change in the shoreline. "Look!" he exclaimed. "An inlet."

He rowed toward it, the boat rising and dipping, rocking and twisting. It felt like a roller coaster ride. Only more frightening. No one ever drowned on a roller coaster.

The water calmed as the boat slid into the inlet. Trees rose above them, sending gnarled branches over the water.

The water here looked black. The boat glided through it silently. Billy remembered the spooky howls and cries he had heard the last time he was here. But this time an eerie quiet had settled over everything.

"Over there." Diana pointed to a spot where the forest floor sloped gently down to the water. The perfect spot to leave the boat.

Billy guided the rowboat to the spot, its bow sliding onto the soft earth. He leapt out of the boat and tied it to a tree.

Diana tossed him the two backpacks, then climbed onto shore.

Billy took a deep breath. The air felt damp and stale. "You ready?"

Diana nodded. Her eyes glowed with determination.

Billy hadn't realized how small the island was. It only took a few minutes before he spotted one of the burned-out beach houses. He and Diana started toward it. As they walked, more of the blackened houses came into view.

"How will we ever find their coffins?" Billy wondered out loud. He glanced at his watch. "It's already afternoon. We should probably split up. It'll be faster."

Diana shifted her backpack. "You really think that's a good idea?"

"You afraid to be alone?"

She hesitated, then nodded. "Yeah, I guess I am. A little. When I killed that vampire Eric on the beach, I was on my own territory. This is different. This is *their* world. It's a lot scarier than a beach."

"Can you still go through with it if we find them?" Billy demanded.

She fixed her gaze on him. "Yes," she declared. "For April."

"It really would be faster if we split up," Billy insisted. "Don't worry. The vampires are asleep. If you find them, all you have to do is call me, and I'll be right there."

Diana nodded. "You're right. I'm sorry. I'm being a wimp." She smiled bravely. "Come on. Let's find Kylie and Irene. I'll go this way. You go that way."

They separated and Billy watched as Diana

stepped into the blackened shell of a cottage. Then he picked out a charred house on his right, strode boldly to the doorway—and stepped inside.

So dark inside. He blinked, eager for his eyes to adjust to the dark.

And realized he was not alone.

Chapter 33

WHO IS IN THE COFFINS?

Billy gasped.

And stared at the face that peered back at him from the shadows.

No time to grab the backpack. No time to pull one of the wooden stakes from the pack.

Billy staggered back—then realized he was staring at a painting.

A large painting, tilted on the charred wall. A woman, open-mouthed, screaming. Her hair flying around her head.

Billy swallowed hard. I just let a painting terrify me, he realized. What am I going to do when I come face to face with a *vampire?*

He studied the painting for a moment. She looks the way I feel, he thought.

He turned away from it, his heart still pounding. Most of the interior walls had been reduced to ashes, so he could see the entire structure from where he stood. Nothing there. Nothing but ashes.

He turned and made his way quickly from the house.

The island was less creepy in the daylight.

But only a little.

Fear made his heart pound and his legs feel weak. But he forced himself to keep moving.

He made his way from house to house. Many had been completely gutted by fire. He searched them quickly, knowing he wouldn't find anything.

He carefully examined any houses that were still intact, peeking into cupboards, peering into closets. No signs of Kylie or Irene.

Where could they be?

He stopped in a small clearing and glanced at his watch. Three forty-five. Billy shook it. It had read three forty-five the last time he looked.

The second hand wasn't moving. The watch had stopped.

How long have I been here? he wondered. How soon does the sun go down?

The rain had stopped, but dark clouds still filled the sky, making it hard to guess the time. Billy figured it must be almost evening. If they didn't find Kylie and Irene soon, they would have to get off the island.

He wondered where Diana was. He had not seen her since they split up.

Billy turned slowly in the clearing, trying to decide on his next move. A distant animal cry, shrill and frightening, floated to him from the woods. The first animal he'd heard since coming ashore.

Does that mean it's almost night? he wondered. Do the animals come out only after dark?

He checked his watch again, just to make sure. Three forty-five.

Should I yell for Diana? he wondered. They still had to make their way back through the trees to the boat.

The boat! Billy thought. Where is it? Which direction is it in?

Suddenly feeling panicked, he let his eyes search the trees. He stood in a small, grass-covered clearing. On one side the grass lay flattened.

Some kind of path?

Yes. Someone had worn a trail there. Recently.

I don't know how long we have before the vampires rise, Billy thought. Should I follow the path, or try to find Diana?

Would the path lead him to the vampires?

Maybe . . .

He followed the path through the woods, knocking branches out of the way. Thick vines grew along the sides. They clung to his skin and clothing as he made his way through.

He stopped in front of a tall tangle of vines and bare tree branches. Thick as a wall.

A wall?

Had someone built this here?

Billy peered through the vines. Yes. He could see something on the other side. He reached into the wall, pushing branches aside.

"Oww!" He cried out as thorns sank into his palm. Billy snatched his hand back and stared at it in horror. Two small dark holes. Deep punctures. Like a vampire bite.

How am I going to get in there? he wondered.

The wall of vines curved around some kind of structure. Protecting it.

This has to be their house, Billy thought. I have to get through.

He pulled a wooden stake from his backpack. Thrust it through the thorns. Working it around, he made a hole large enough to see through.

Yes! A house.

A charred house behind the wall of vines.

It was burned, but not badly. The walls and roof appeared to be solid. Working furiously,

Billy enlarged the hole until it was big enough for him to crawl through, then put away the stake.

Thorns snagged his backpack and clothes, leaving long scratches on his skin. He ignored them. He didn't take his eyes off the burned-out house.

Billy glanced up at the sky. The rain had stopped. The clouds moved quickly, as if a strong wind were blowing them.

How soon till sunset? he wondered. How much time do I have?

He ran to the door of the house. He grabbed the knob. It turned easily. The door swung open about an inch, then stopped. Something on the inside was holding it closed.

Billy pushed. The door opened a little farther. He shoved it with all his strength. Whatever blocked the door scraped across the floor.

The door stood open about a foot. Billy squeezed through the opening.

Total darkness, except for the light from the open door.

Billy waited for his eyes to adjust. The first thing he was able to see was a dresser that had been shoved against the door.

Slowly the room came into focus. Billy stood in what had been the kitchen. It smelled stale, like an old campfire.

His eyes darted around the room. He couldn't see much. The room seemed to be completely bare.

Billy stepped through the doorway into the next room. It was even darker here, damp and musty. Deep shadows crept from the corners, pools of blackness that seemed to absorb the dim light spilling in from the kitchen.

He examined the walls. Someone had nailed boards over the windows.

From the inside.

Billy peered around the room, trying to see into the shadows.

"Whoa," he whispered. In the corner. What was that?

The shadows were so deep that Billy could barely make out the three shapes. He moved quickly across the room—and saw three long, rectangular boxes.

Coffins.

Billy's breath caught in his throat. A wave of terror swept over him, holding him in place, holding his eyes on the coffins.

Yes. Yes. I have found what I am looking for, he told himself. I have found the resting place of the vampires.

But when does the sun go down? Do I have enough time to destroy them before they awaken?

Billy stared at the coffins, his pulse racing.

I cannot stand here gaping. I have to look inside, he told himself.

He took a deep breath. Reached out with trembling hands. And lifted the lid on the coffin closest to him.

Chapter 34

HAMMER TIME

Billy tugged the coffin lid up. Forced himself to stare inside.

Girls' clothes.

Nothing but clothes.

He picked up a short skirt, a midriff top. He rummaged around, sifting through bathing suits and jeans.

Did the clothing belong to Kylie and Irene? Some of it did look familiar.

Had he found Kylie and Irene's coffins? Had he been lucky enough to find the right place?

Open the other coffins, Billy instructed himself. Hurry! You've got to see. You've got to know.

The remaining two coffins rested end-to-end, only a couple of inches apart.

Billy grabbed both lids at once, one in each hand.

With a hard tug, he yanked the lids up. Then he bent to peer inside.

Trembling, his breath coming in ragged gasps, Billy stared into the coffins.

Kylie and Irene.

Yes.

Sound asleep. Eyes shut. Faces calm, at peace.

Sleeping in ancient dirt.

Hands folded across their chests.

Billy stared at them, swallowing hard. Stared as if he'd never seen them before.

They appeared so innocent.

Kylie stirred, shifted her position slightly. She smacked her lips, revealing the tips of her fangs. Dreaming of food? Billy wondered. Dreaming of human blood? *My* blood?

Don't stand there! a voice inside Billy screamed. *Time is running out! Do something! Before it's too late!*

But the sight of them seemed to hold him in place. He couldn't take his eyes off them. Kylie with her beautiful red hair. Irene's golden curls glowing even in the dim light.

Billy stared at them, stared without moving, without breathing—as if the two vampires were able to cloud his mind even in their sleep.

Snap out of it! he warned himself.

Billy blinked, shook his head.

Hurry!

Frantically, Billy slipped off the backpack and tossed it to the floor. He ripped at the cloth, unable to get it open.

I've got to calm down, he thought. Calm down.

The zipper tore. The bag fell open, spilling wooden stakes onto the floor. Billy snatched one up and grabbed the hammer.

Gasping for breath, he held the pointed tip of the oak stake over Kylie's heart. Extra-hard wood. Sharpened to a point as deadly as the tips of Kylie's fangs.

Billy's hands shook so hard he wasn't sure he could swing the hammer. Or hit the stake with it.

Can I do this? he wondered. Can I really do this?

He raised the hammer.

Chapter 35

BREAKFAST

Billy raised the hammer. It felt so heavy in his trembling hand. As if it weighed a hundred pounds.

He lowered it.

I can't do this, he thought. I can't pound a pointed stake into a person's chest.

He peered down at Kylie.

She's not a person, Billy told himself. She used to be a person. But now she's a deadly vampire. She could be a thousand years old!

And how many innocent people has she murdered in all her years?

He took a deep breath. Once again, he leaned over Kylie and placed the tip of the stake in the center of her chest.

He positioned the hammer over the stake. He raised the hammer. Held it shakily over the stake.

Counted silently to three.

And Kylie opened her eyes.

"Oh!" Billy uttered a shocked cry and staggered back. The hammer and stake fell from his hands and clattered loudly on the floor.

Kylie sat up, instantly alert. Her eyes narrowed on Billy.

An angry hiss escaped her throat. "Billy . . ." she whispered. "Billy . . ."

The whisper appeared to wake Irene. She sat up alertly, wide awake in an instant, and gazed at Billy.

Billy took another step back. He opened his mouth to speak. But realized he had nothing to say.

"Billy . . ." Kylie whispered, a smile spreading across her face. "Billy . . ."

"Billy . . ." Irene echoed in a harsh whisper. "Billy . . ."

The two vampires floated up from their coffins.

"Billy . . . Billy . . ."

He tried to run—but stumbled over the hammer and went tumbling into the wall.

"Billy . . . Billy . . ."

They floated over him, both chanting his name.

"Billy . . ." Kylie whispered in his ear.

She ran her tongue over her lips. "Billy . . . so glad you decided to drop in for breakfast."

Chapter 36

KYLIE'S TURN

Irene held one arm. Kylie gripped the other.

Billy struggled frantically to free himself.

"Billy . . . give up, Billy," Irene whispered. "You can't get away from us. We are stronger than you can possibly imagine."

Billy ignored her. He fought desperately, twisting, turning. But their fingers dug into his flesh, their powerful grip unbreakable.

He took a deep breath, pulled back his arms—and shoved Kylie with all his strength.

She stumbled, letting go.

He swung his whole body, slamming Irene with his shoulder.

Her grip loosened. Only a tiny bit. But enough.

Billy whirled to his left.

He was free!

"You're strong for a mortal," Irene growled. "But not strong enough." She lunged for him.

Billy turned, started to run—and tripped over the backpack.

He fell hard, landing on his elbows and knees.

Wooden stakes clattered across the floor in all directions.

The vampires floated over him, hissing and drooling.

Their eyes glowed with rage, with hunger.

Irene sprang at him.

Billy rolled to the left. His fingers wrapped around one of the stakes. He snatched it up.

Irene flew down on him, her fangs aimed at his throat.

And Billy shoved the stake up toward her chest.

He closed his eyes.

Irene's weight crashed down on him.

I missed, he realized. I missed her heart.

I'm dead.

Silence for a moment.

And then Irene let out a piercing howl. As Billy opened his eyes, she flew to her feet. Then she staggered backward, the wooden stake jutting from her chest.

No blood, Billy saw. Not a drop.

Irene screamed. She tossed back her head in a long howl of pain.

And as she howled, she began to age.

Her hair turned white.

Her face wrinkled and sagged.

As Billy stared in amazement, Irene's hair fell out, until nothing remained but a few white wisps, wriggling like snakes on her pink scalp.

Irene collapsed to the floor.

Her legs shriveled to stumps. Her face caved in. The skin flaked off, revealing gray bone.

Her screams continued from her open-jawed skull.

And then the skull crumbled into dust.

And the room was silent.

Billy stared at the puddle of dust on the floor.

Kylie's shriek of rage made him spin around.

She grabbed Billy under the shoulders and lifted him off his feet.

"My turn," she whispered. "My turn."

Chapter 37

KYLIE HAS EYES FOR BILLY

Kylie's nails dug into Billy's skin. He felt the hot tips of her fangs on his neck.

"Billy!" Diana's voice. From outside. "Billy, the sun is setting! We have to go!"

Still holding Billy, Kylie spun around in a circle, her long red hair flying behind her. "Who is that?" she demanded.

Diana burst into the room. "Billy!" she screamed.

Kylie whirled to face Diana. "April—what are you doing here?"

"Let him down!" Diana cried.

"But, April—" Kylie protested. "You're one of us. Why are you helping Billy?"

"I'm not April—and I'm not one of you," Diana told her.

Kylie's eyes flashed. "You will be," she snapped. "As soon as I finish with him." Her fangs slid down all the way as she lowered her face to Billy's throat.

Billy's hand shot out. With all his strength he held Kylie away. Her fangs hovered inches from his throat.

Kylie's face twisted with rage. She snapped her jaws like an animal, trying to sink her fangs into the soft flesh of Billy's neck.

With a terrified gasp, Billy raised his right hand—and jabbed two fingers into Kylie's eyes.

"Yeowwwwwww!" She opened her mouth in a howl of pain.

Her hands flew up to her eyes. Billy plunged to the floor.

Howling, Kylie covered her eyes with both hands.

Billy turned and saw Diana at the window. "Now, die!" Diana shrieked at Kylie. "Die! Die!"

With a cry of rage, Diana ripped a board off the window.

A bright square of afternoon sunlight slanted into the room.

The orange light washed over Kylie.

She never uncovered her eyes.

As her skin began to shrivel and peel off, she

held her eyes tightly, bending in pain, howling, howling.

Until her head rolled off her body. Her body tumbled to the floor, across the square of orange light, melting, flaking, shriveling.

To dust.

Billy swallowed hard, staring in disbelief as Kylie's body fell apart. Only the eyeballs remained, staring up accusingly at him.

Staring. Staring. Until they too melted and became wet, green puddles on the floor.

"It's over," Billy said with a sigh, moving quickly across the room to Diana. "It's over." He hugged her, hugged her tightly.

They stood there, still shivering, still trembling, hugging until the sun disappeared behind the trees.

Chapter 38

THE PARTY IS OVER

"Come on," Diana urged, dragging Billy into the Pizza Cove.

It was nearly ten o'clock, and the place was still packed. Kids were talking and laughing and gobbling down pizza. Billy spotted an empty booth in the corner, and they slid into it.

Billy felt upset because Jay was still so weak. Jay's parents had taken him home so the family doctor could examine him.

"I don't know what's going to happen to him," Billy told Diana. "Kylie never finished turning him into a vampire. But he's so weak. And he never seems to get any better."

"Jay will get well," Diana assured him, as she studied the menu. "Now that he's away from here."

"I hope you're right," Billy told her.

"Cheer up," Diana said brightly. "We did it. We destroyed the vampires. We won!"

"We only destroyed two of them," Billy replied glumly.

"I can't believe you're acting like this," Diana scolded.

He managed a laugh. "You're right. I should be happy. What kind of pizza do you want?"

"Pepperoni with lots of green peppers."

They ordered it.

Billy watched the waiters scurry back and forth, taking orders and delivering steaming pizzas.

The tangy aroma of baking pizzas from the big ovens in back filled the restaurant.

Finally the waiter delivered their order. "Enjoy," he told them, as he set down the steaming pie and two plates.

"Give me your plate," Diana told him. "You get the honor of having the first slice."

Billy didn't want any pizza, but he handed her his plate.

"Uh-oh," Diana complained. "They didn't cut it all the way through." She fumbled with a slice of pizza, twisting it this way and that, but it refused to come loose.

"Let me," Billy offered. He picked up a knife from the table.

He pulled the pizza over to his side of the table. Inserted the blade into the pie, and pulled the knife toward him.

"Oww." The blade slid off the pan—and sliced into Billy's finger.

A bad cut. A deep one. Billy tried to hide it.

Too late. Diana had seen it.

She stared at him, her mouth open, eyes wide. "Billy—no blood," she cried. "Such a deep cut, and there was no blood."

"I'm sorry you saw that," Billy told her.

Diana leapt up with a startled cry.

But Billy grabbed her wrist. He pulled her back down into her seat.

"Let me explain," he pleaded, not letting go of Diana. "I lied about working on a charter boat. During the day, I'm asleep in my coffin. Direct sunlight will kill me. I can go out in daylight only if it's dark and cloudy—like when we went to the island and killed Kylie and Irene."

Diana stared at him in silent horror.

"I missed a whole year of school," Billy explained. "My friends all thought I was in the hospital. But I had to sleep in my coffin every day."

"A vampire," Diana whispered. "You're a vampire."

"It happened here in Sandy Hollow last summer," Billy explained. His voice cracked with emotion. "Last summer. That's when they turned me into a vampire."

"If you're a vampire," Diana demanded, "why did you help me kill two others?"

"To pay back the vampires. To pay them back for turning me into one of *them.* I hate them for making me crave the nectar. I killed Mae-Linn. For the nectar. I needed it so badly. I couldn't help myself. And I killed that guy Rick, too. I was so hungry!"

Diana shook her head. "It can't be," she whispered. "It can't be!"

"Now you know everything, Diana," Billy whispered. "Now I have no secrets. And I'm so hungry. So terribly hungry."

Diana cried out.

Too late.

Billy pulled her close. He sank his fangs deep into her throat.

Screams of terror filled the restaurant.

Billy barely heard them.

He was so hungry.

So terribly hungry.

About the Author

"Where do you get your ideas?"

That's the question that R. L. Stine is asked most often. "I don't know where my ideas come from," he says. "But I do know that I have a lot more scary stories in my mind that I can't wait to write."

So far, he has written over a hundred mysteries and thrillers for young people, all of them bestsellers.

Bob grew up in Columbus, Ohio. Today he lives in an apartment near Central Park in New York City with his wife, Jane, and son, Matt.